Take Time

The Robinswood Press

FOREWORDS

Take Time is a very useful book as it not only outlines the area of difficulty that children with learning problems so often encounter, but gives specific exercise sheets to cover each aspect. There are not many books on spatiality, body awareness and movement which also incorporate activities to improve the child's performance, and I am sure that therapists involved with learning difficulties will find it invaluable.

The bean bag exercises are particularly well described and illustrated and link in well with the rhythm and timing suggestions mentioned earlier.

Sequencing seems to be a perennial problem, and there are many suggestions for helping here; such simple things as threading beads in colour order to learning the months of the year, the alphabet and on to times tables.

To my mind no therapist or teacher of Specific Learning Difficulties should be without this edition by their side.

Dr Beve Hornsby PhD., MSc., MEd., F.R.C.S.L.T., A.F.B.Ps.S.
Consultant Speech and Language Therapist, Clinical
Psychologist, and Principal of The Hornsby International
Centre, London.

Delays in the development of body image, co-ordination and the perception of one's self in space are, in some cases, related to language and concomitant educational difficulties. A child must be able to recognise the direction of his body in three dimensional space in order to be able to interpret the direction of two dimensional symbols.

Drawing on her experience as a curative eurythmist, Miss Hunt has designed exercises to aid the general development of the unco-ordinated, poorly orientated, clumsy child.

Although they seem deceptively simple, the application of the exercises requires a degree of planning on the part of the teacher using them so that the complex goals are achieved. Because there are no published standards by which to measure a particular child's performance, the importance of recording individual progress for each case must be stressed; comparing the 'before' and 'after' abilities serves as a monitor of the efficacy of the therapy.

The exercises have been developed in the Learning Disabilities Clinic over a number of years and were found to be very useful both in refining deficiencies in performance and providing an important element in the overall remedial programme designed for each child.

This is an interesting book and I am glad to see the link up between language and movement combined.

Dr Alan MacAuslan M.A., M.B.B.Chir.
Retired Director, Learning Difficulties Clinic, St Thomas'
Hospital, London.

AUTHORS' NOTE

For Everyone:

Children who still have difficulties with speaking, reading, writing or spelling may be helped by tackling one of the many possible root causes: lack of co-ordination, rhythm and timing.

Take Time, as the title suggests, means devoting a few minutes every day to the development of a child's concentration and confidence, balance and control. This book indicates what points to watch for in a child whose specific needs are often overlooked. It outlines a programme of special exercises designed to be not only functional but fun. Carefully chosen and cheerfully used, these should help even the most awkward child to improve.

For Therapists and Teachers:

Movement can be recognised as a fundamental activity of life. It is perceived in liveliness of thinking, in the fluctuations of feeling and human interaction and most obviously in the physical body.

This recognition has given rise to a hypothesis regarding the therapeutic potential of movement. Therapeutically, it should be possible to correct abnormal movement patterns in any dimension by exercises which emphasise healthy and appropriate movements. This should also be possible for some difficulties in the emotional and cognitive functions.

We have taken exercises from the fields of Speech and Language Therapy and Eurythmy which are appropriate to the cognitive and motor problems associated with speech, reading and writing. These exercises have proved to be of a very fundamental and elementary nature; they aim to help a child establish a connection between his inner world and the outer world. A child will show many of his problems in the way he moves and carries out an action: such problems include poor balance, lack of co-ordination, lack of rhythmic sense, lack of directional sense, uncertainty and fatigue. By working in an imaginative way with the child, his dexterity, ability to move and even inner cognitive agility can be helped. These exercises focus on movement, rhythm, form and direction.

Our thanks go wholeheartedly to Miss Audrey McAllen (Consultant Specific Learning Difficulties Teacher), whose consistent encouragement and enthusiasm has inspired us; Miss Diane Flowers (Eurythmist and Artist), who illustrated the exercises; and to all those who encouraged us to set down for a wider readership this tried-and-tested programme of exercises that has proved so rewarding in helping children to overcome their difficulties.

Mary Nash-Wortham M.R.C.S.L.T., Dip.Sp.L.D.,
and Jean Hunt Dip.LSEu.

SECTION A

Introduction

EQUIPMENT

Bits and pieces required to complete the Pointers and Exercises.

- *Balls*, two tennis balls or similar soft but firm variety, both of the same size.

- *Beads* (big ones), plus suitable thread and mixed buttons for sorting into groups.

- *Bean bags*, two home made ones are best, size 10-15cm (4½ - 6 inch square), filled with split peas or rice, covered in soft, nice to touch material (velvet off-cuts are ideal) in clear colours, for example, blue and red.

- *Blu-tack*, or other adhesive.

- *Cardboard*, large white sheets (up to 4 may be required), available from stationers.

- *Crayons*, wax or soft, easy-to-use variety.

- *Drawing paper*, unlined, any quality, good size.

- *Felt tip pens*, mixed colours.

- *Floor markers*, ten small drink mats, large plastic counters, buttons or pebbles.

- *Kaleidoscope*, if available, no need to buy one.

- *Lined paper*, and a full sized pencil with sharpened lead.

- *Mirror*, hold-in-the-hand size.

- *Paint brush*, child's size with a good brush.

- *Scissors*, blunt or rounded ends.

- *Shoe-laces*, in a shoe for lacing and tying.

- *Skipping rope*, with wooden handles so that the rope turns easily.

- *Ribbons*, in three different colours for bow tying and plaiting (mainly for girls).

- *Rod*, 2cm diameter wood doweling 43cm (15 inches) long, or even better: a similar length of copper rod.

- *Tie*, necktie (mainly for boys).

- *Tambourine*, triangle or drum to make rhythmic beat music.

QUESTIONS

Why should a child aged 5-6 upwards find it hard to:

- *talk* clearly and in constructive sentences?

- *say* long words without ending up in a muddle?

- *find* the right word to describe an object?

- *hold* a pencil comfortably and easily?

- *write* clearly with letters and numbers facing the right way?

- *read* sounds and words which are really there?

If a child cannot handle such frustrating and apparently insoluble problems, he or she may also find it difficult to:

- *crawl* along the floor without losing the normal rhythm of arm and opposite knee going forward together.

- *sit* still on a chair for more than a minute at a time.

- *walk* along a painted or chalked straight line without losing balance.

- *run* fast into a sprint.

- *skip*, probably not at all with a rope.

- *hop* more than once or twice on one leg without giving up.

- *jump* small jumps with both feet really together, without tumbling over.

- *throw* and catch a ball by judgement rather than by luck.

- *hold* a knife and fork in the correct hands without fumbling or dropping them.

- *eat* nicely.

- *dress* in an orderly fashion: look tidy and smart, for a short while at least.

COMMENTS. Different sorts of specialist help.

The child in question who has these difficulties may present you with an area of concern which perhaps nobody else seems to appreciate. If there is no easy solution or known remedy, other people's interest in the problem wears thin very rapidly. "He'll grow out of it."; "Needs time to mature."; "Slow developer." and "Lazy." are all familiar responses.

Take a positive approach.

Before embarking on any programme of exercises, if the child is already receiving help from a *specialist*, ask his advice about whether exercises would be helpful.

Make sure the child's *hearing* and *eyesight* have been checked at pre-school check-up or during the first year at school.

If in doubt, ask your own Doctor or Health Visitor who will arrange for a hearing test to be carried out or arrange the referral to any other specialist source and advise you accordingly.

HEARING

Hearing loss can be small but specific, for example affecting high frequency sounds only, so although hearing is adequate for everyday life, it is just down enough to affect specific listening needed for word building and spelling.

EYESIGHT

Colour blindness can be identified. It is useful to know whether a child is colour blind or not; the Class Teacher likes to know as well.

Visual field defects are harder to spot. Some children can see perfectly well, but when scanning a page of print (at close range) the vision cuts off or distorts a part, although when looking further away, the visual field is perfectly normal. An Optometrist can help with special tests and exercises.

An Optician cannot 'solve' reading problems with glasses if a child has perfect eyesight; but glasses can help with the focus and clarity of print on the page. Tinted (coloured) lenses or overlays on the printed page can prove beneficial too.

SPECIALIST SOURCES

Psychologists (Child, Educational or Clinical Psychologist) see children by special request from Head Teachers at school, or through a Doctor at the Health Centre or Hospital. A variety of graded tests provide a guide to the child's intelligence, and pin-point areas of particular difficulty. Advice is given on the right kind of help needed.

Speech and Language Therapists see children upon direct request from many sources, including concerned parents. They are able to diagnose and programme treatment required from start to finish, either alone, or with Psychologists, Physiotherapists, Occupational Therapists, Specialist Gymnasts, Special Needs Teachers and additional specialised expertise, which in a combined programme makes up a multi-discipline approach.

Multi-Discipline assessments can be given at many major hospital-based centres throughout the country, where specialists can work as a team from one unit.

Special Needs or Learning Support, are teachers who should have attended additional training courses to equip them to be aware of the many different types of difficulties children encounter, and have teaching methods available to help the individual child, using a one-to-one teaching method (seeing the child alone), teaching in a small selected group, or giving specific help in and during a normal classroom lesson.

Eurythmy Therapists work with total activity of the body as a whole in three dimensional space, relating the gross movements to fine control required for reading and writing in two dimensional space.

Art Therapists help children through painting (flow) and modelling work (form and shape).

There are others who may also contribute towards assessment and help. These include music therapists and the increasingly available and acceptable fields of natural medicine and treatment, including homoeopathic doctors, practitioners of specific massage, reflexology and craniology. Always check their qualifications, their fees, and exactly what they offer.

This drawing by an intelligent boy of 8 years 6 months shows how he has difficulty with perception of shape, proportion, and definition.

SPECIFIC LABELS. Diagnostic Terms.

'DYSPRAXIA' or 'DYSLEXIA'?

Confusion can best be unscrambled by considering the 'unfolding' nature of dyspraxia as the range of problems experienced becomes wider and more evident as the child progresses, and more is expected in each succeeding stage, both at home and at school, socially and scholastically. This has considerable impact not only for the child, but also for the family who are trying to help.

Dyslexia relates to a much more definable area which can be seen as real trouble with letter recognition, shape and direction, always spelling and often reading. This may link into *dyscalculia* or difficulty with numbers, concepts of size and shape, calculations, sequencing required for times tables, and inevitably the need for quick memory recall, apart from the difficulty of actually reading the questions and unpicking the problems.

The dyslexic child may have difficulties which overlap with the dyspraxic, the dyscalculic, and indeed there are a few more 'dys' areas; these are defined by careful professional assessment, but it really is best to remember that a 'label' does not mean a life sentence, it just means action is needed to improve matters!

The indicators for *verbal dyspraxia* are those associated with making and co-ordinating the very precise movements of over one hundred muscles which come together to make the speech apparatus work in unison to create clear articulation.

The *speech apparatus* includes the lips, the tongue tip, blade and back which pushes against the soft part of the palate; the soft palate closes off the nasal airways used for blowing, sucking, swallowing, and for speaking the /m/ /n/ and /ng/ sounds, also for resonance and tone of the voice.

The 'voice' or sound is created in the central neck region of the larynx, which again depends upon the muscles controlling breath. This has to be both sufficient and controlled enough to synchronise the air passing through the vocal folds in a series of rapid puffs which cause the sound of 'voice' through vibration.

Normal speech is, therefore, entirely dependent upon breath control from the lungs, passing through the vocal folds to make sound, which is turned into meaningful speech by the rapid movements of the soft palate, tongue and lips, the position of the jaws and teeth, and the resonance of the whole process in the hollow sinus regions of the neck and head.

The *dyspraxic* child may be found to have one or more of the following difficulties:

- Speech sounds are omitted, unclear or substituted.

- Sequencing sounds may be distorted with substitutions or omissions.

- Sentences are unclear, incomplete, often grammatically flawed.

- Speed, pace, rhythm and loudness of speech can be unusual, distorted, or abnormal.

- Feeding, as a baby, and later with chewing will often prove to be slow, hard going.

- Swallowing in gulps, sometimes dribbling may be apparent.

Dyspraxic children often have a history of delayed onset of speech, and a continuing delay in speech (use of words) and language (use of sentences, and structure of sentences). It is not unusual for dyspraxic children to start single word talking age as late as three or four years, progress may be slow, and grammatical errors often persist long into Junior school.

Verbal Dyspraxia may be the only problem for the child, or it may be associated with a range of other symptoms, including some of the following:

- *Attention Deficit Disorders ('ADD')* ranging from quite severe hyper-activity, behaviour problems, attention seeking, to milder forms of short concentration, poor memory, and forgetfulness.

- *Clumsiness* ranging from the odd trip-up to real difficulty with dressing, looking neat and staying that way; disorganisation which affects daily living and upsets all those around at home and school.

Associated closely with verbal dyspraxia is:

i) the inability to write clearly, which can be linked to the physical difficulty of actually holding and co-ordinating the fine movements of the writing implement.

ii) a link (often overlooked as such) with the verbal language problem when the actual processing and formation of words into a meaningful flow of ideas and thoughts from the brain to the mouth (where spoken expression takes place), or to the writing hand (where the composition takes place as written expression) is confused.

A pupil who has difficulty with spelling and number order of letters and figures, difficulty with writing ideas down clearly on to paper, often has an associated but possibly less evident verbal language weakness too; beware the silent, quiet, seldom heard pupil, who covers up his verbal limitations with a reserved attitude, and even a stammer to help prevent the necessity of direct attention. Verbal dyspraxia can be a hidden handicap as well as the very obvious one which you can 'see' as soon as the child tumbles into the room!

DYSPRAXIA FROM THE EURYTHMIST'S PERSPECTIVE

Normally, early childhood development follows an orderly, predictable inter-related sequence, which is directly related to a child's intellectual and learning capabilities. Each developmental stage assimilates part of the previous one, so full function is dependent on the level achieved in the stage below. Logical conclusions may be drawn to show that children's learning and behaviour may be affected if any of the natural developmental stages of early childhood are omitted, with laterality (or sidedness) being the final stage of development in the central nervous system.

'Dyspraxia' is to do with movement. In the adjustment or release of total movement comes fine motor control. It could be that primal reflexes have not been released in the very young child. Any infant in its first few months can perform any basic movement. The potential is there. Tired, exhausted children stem from too early an introduction to head learning (brain work). Television for example and computers at too young an age, not understood and mastered, but used as play things, attractions or diversions, can be detrimental to normal development, and children can become adult too soon. Lack of natural play stops the inter-connection between inner and outer activity. Therefore, what they are learning cannot become 'imprinted' or stay in the brain.

To help find these underdeveloped skills, the child with co-ordination difficulties has to experience for himself how to balance, move, speak and then to give or respond through expression. The developmental exercises in Section D, many based on the figure of '8', are to help the child experience and practise working through both sides of the body and both hemispheres of the brain. The crucial crossing over point in the centre of the '8' encourages freedom of movement from one hemisphere to the other enabling the brain to use both sides of the body in harmony.

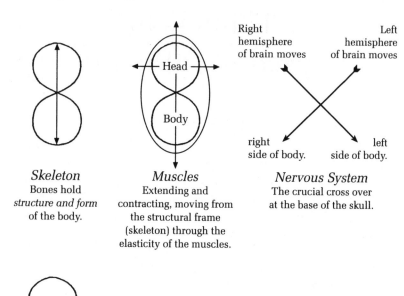

Skeleton
Bones hold *structure and form* of the body.

Muscles
Extending and contracting, moving from the structural frame (skeleton) through the elasticity of the muscles.

Nervous System
The crucial cross over at the base of the skull.

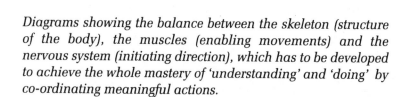

Upright figure of 8 brings in consciousness of standing, balance, walking.

Sideways mid-line crossing develops left/right movement and links with writing.

Diagrams showing the balance between the skeleton (structure of the body), the muscles (enabling movements) and the nervous system (initiating direction), which has to be developed to achieve the whole mastery of 'understanding' and 'doing' by co-ordinating meaningful actions.

SECTION B

Pointers to
Areas of Difficulty

POINTER 1 Timing and Rhythm.

So many children have timing and rhythm troubles; rhythm in melody and words is strongly marked and yet many children find it difficult to:

- *sing* a simple nursery rhyme in time and in tune.

- *clap* the rhythm of the nursery rhyme accurately.

- *walk* out the rhythm of a nursery rhyme, using the whole room to do it.

- *clap* in time to a simple tune.

- *march* round the room in time to a tune. Arms as well as legs should swing evenly and synchronise with the whole body as well as with the music.

Rhythm is a basic pre-learning skill because a child who gabbles or who reads in a monotonous voice often fails to assimilate what he reads. Help with his disorganisation of speech-rhythm may well assist his reading skill.

By getting the child to step out rhythmically the metre of a poem, the helper can introduce the child to a flow of sound and its related movement. This requires of the child accurate listening and attention. Many related skills are therefore introduced and developed simultaneously.

When the child has the poem 'in his limbs', we hope the end result will be that he can write the poem down (a further related movement skill) and then read back his own work aloud. This leads the child into a natural linking process of body awareness, memory through movement, agile thinking, and an inward understanding of what he is reading aloud by hearing his own words.

Use Exercise Sheet 1 for Pointer 1.   Page 40

POINTER 2 Direction and Goal.

Directional problems are usually quite easy to detect in a child. Left hand turning and right hand turning, though easy for some, can be dreadfully confusing for others. Following instructions becomes a nightmare, especially if the child is in a hurry. One simple instruction at a time may be all that he can assimilate. Even the older child, who is always late or turning up in the wrong place, finds himself an unwitting target for his peers' jokes.

Some disorientated children find it extremely difficult to read or write continuously in the same direction; they skip words, or jump lines. Many others twist hands, arms or whole bodies while writing – instead of organising the direction of the activity from within themselves. Similar problems occur when these gross body movements are transferred to the fine movements of visual perception, and we see the child writing /f/ instead of /t/ and /d/ instead of /b/.

Here again, exercises can develop a more coherent strategy of movement and direction, by developing the kinaesthetic sense which underlines the processes of speech, reading and writing. Such exercises help the child re-align and re-assemble his disturbed or weak movement patterns and learn to distinguish between up-down, left-right and the diagonal crossing of the midline.

It is through awareness and control of the chaotic movement or fixed form that a balance can be brought about. The effort required by the child's helper will either awaken his ability to direct his activities from within or to release tension which prevents his response to outer stimuli.

As a simple test:

Ask the child to repeat clearly after you each command before carrying it out:

- "Show me your left hand." (Relax)
- "Put your left hand up." (Relax)
- "Put your left hand over your right hand." (Relax)
- "Put your left hand on your right ear." (Relax)
- "Stand up. Turn around to the left." (Relax)

Make sure the child clearly understands each command before trying it. Note how many sections of a command the child can assimilate then carry out correctly.

Use Exercise Sheet 2 for Pointer 2.   Page 43

POINTER 3 Spatial Orientation and Movement.

SPATIAL ORIENTATION

Spatial Orientation, or forms in space, must be mastered before a child can hope to get down to shapes and forms which create letters on paper.

MOVEMENT

The child must make an inner action to bring about the outward movement; this requires imagination and the ability to move from inner to outer. It is the helper's task to stimulate this inner activity by giving the child a verbal picture of the form. It is important to understand that the helper does not draw the form on the floor for the child, as this would make the movement a mere outward, cognitive-based action, not derived from the child's inner awareness of himself in space.

The symbols used in reading and writing are based on two forms – the curve and the straight line. When the body has learned to recognise and move along these shapes, the refined movements of hand-eye co-ordination can be developed. The child consciously makes the shapes come into existence with his body. Full consciousness of these shapes is produced in movement with the child walking the form with his body facing in the same direction all the time.

As an example, the older child (6-7 years onwards) who walks the boundary of an imagined triangle, while facing the same wall, gains a fuller experience of his orientation in space (left/right, forward/backward) than the child who walks a triangular path always moving forwards, turning his body at the corners of the triangle.

To produce the form using the first method is more difficult, but it is what should happen in writing; the body should remain still, even the arm and hand should have very little movement, it must be the inner activity which brings about the outer movement.

Movement Exercise – for close observation and assessment purposes. The helper should demonstrate the movement exercise to the child first.

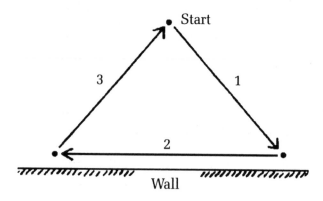

Keep eyes forward looking at one point on the wall ahead, then

1   step diagonally left forwards, then

2   step sideways horizontally to the right, then

3   step backwards diagonally to the left, returning to the beginning point.

NORMAL SPATIAL ORIENTATION AGE GUIDE IN YEARS

Age   As a simple diagnostic test, ask the child to:

3-4
- draw an imaginary circle in the air with one hand and arm.

- draw a circle on plain paper with a crayon.

- walk or run a large imaginary circle around the floor, as though going around the edge of a large puddle.

- draw an imaginary cross in the air with one hand and arm.

- draw a cross on plain paper with a crayon.

4-5
- draw an imaginary cross in the air with one hand and arm.

- draw a square on plain paper with a crayon.

- walk a large imaginary square shape out on the floor, each corner turned 90° with precision, turning into each direction.

5-6
- draw an imaginary triangle in the air with one hand and arm.

- draw a triangle on plain paper with a crayon.

- walk an imaginary triangle shape out on the floor, starting with the base line, following the line of direction.

6-7
- draw an imaginary diamond shape in the air with one hand and arm.

- draw a diamond on plain paper with a crayon.

If all these tests are achieved easily, the next step is to see if the child can draw a simple free form on the blackboard or paper using very simple joined straight lines and curves, beginning with a straight line, and a curve. Can the child then "walk the path" he has drawn? Ask the child to "walk the path" he has just drawn and observe the results closely. Can he remember the pattern without referring back to the blackboard or paper?

Use Exercise Sheet 3 for Pointer 3.   Page 48

POINTER 4 Sequencing.

Direction, Spatial Orientation and Sequencing are linked. Many children seem unable to follow the right order or sequence of words, figures or letters. They reverse the usual run or flow of certain shapes, patterns and ideas.

NORMAL ACHIEVEMENT AGE GUIDE IN YEARS

Age   Can the child tell you:

3-4   • his *own name* aloud correctly, including *surname*?

4-5   • *name* and *address*?

5-6   • *name*, *address* and *telephone number*?
        • the *numbers* from 1-10 correctly?
        • the days of the week?

6-7   • his *birthday*, *date* and *month*, and say it aloud?

7-8   • the *months* of the year in the correct order?
        • the four *seasons* of the year in the correct sequence?
        • the *numbers* from 1-10, then 10-1 without missing any?
        • *numbers* aloud in 2, 4, 6, 8, steps up to 24?
        • the *time*?

Can the child:

• draw the face of the *clock* with numbers in the correct positions?

• write his *address* and *telephone number* down?

• draw a simple *compass cross* marking on the four points, North, South, East and West?

If the child cannot sequence naturally, then putting letters in correct order for spelling becomes a mammoth ordeal for him; sometimes difficulty with numbers, times tables and arithmetic presents problems, too. This is an additional hazard linked with sequencing.

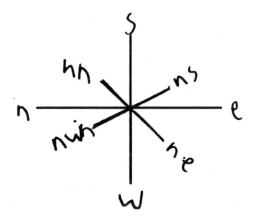

An example of an 8 year old pupil enthusiastically and neatly drawing and labelling compass points, certain that he had got it all just right.

Use Exercise Sheet 4 for Pointer 4. Page 61

POINTER 5 Fine Motor Control for Speech, Writing and Reading.

(Or highly controlled small movements.)

Fine motor control is needed for speech, writing and reading.

SPEECH

Lots of children can speak fairly clearly but some get tied up with a difficult or less familiar word and hurriedly swap it for an easier one. Some breathe through the mouth only, or chew food badly and drink in gulps. Some talk in a rush, so that it is hard to understand what they are saying.

WRITING

Lots of children can paint pictures but cannot hold a slim pencil comfortably. Lots of children can manage big untidy writing, but not neat, clearly legible letters.

READING

Lots of children can read a sentence or two, really very nicely, then they come to a faltering, grinding halt, or their reading turns into a gabble, with more and more mistakes.

Only in human beings are the highly developed minuscule movements of the voice, soft palate, tongue, teeth and lips so accurately synthesised giving the ability to produce speech. Likewise, by the smooth flow of thought down to the finger tips clasping the quickly moving pen in a series of tiny movements, people have mastered the written word. The left to right movement of the eyes over the printed page for seeing, photographing and instantly transporting the printed message to the brain, where it is decoded into comprehension, is also a gift to man alone. To some children, however, it is a misery of struggling; to see the print but be unable to interpret it as quickly or as accurately as others do is both frustrating and demoralising.

Exercises can greatly improve controlled movement when started when the child is young enough, and further progress comes with practice and maturity.

Illustrations by a boy, aged 8 years 6 months, with above average intelligence, but marked speech, reading and writing problems, which are resolving, as can be seen by his contribution on page 28.

Use Exercise Sheet 5 for Pointer 5.

Page 65

POINTER 6 Laterality.

(Or which side of the body?)

Laterality is an important milestone towards establishing strong sided brain function (or secondary laterality) which can be shown to relate to reading, writing and spelling. Sometimes the words 'crossed lateral' crop up. Some research suggests that as many as 43% of the population are crossed lateral. Although it has not made any apparent difference to most people (and in fact they may not even know they are) there is growing evidence to support the view that 'laterality', or which hand, eye, ear and foot are used, if confused by a mixture of perhaps right hand, left eye and right leg, can account for language based difficulties and the more obvious symptoms related to spelling disorder and reading delay. If this is the case, then it is helpful to know and understand if a child does use the right hand, eye and foot side, or the left hand, eye and foot side, or a mixture of both and is therefore crossed lateral, sometimes called 'mixed dominance'.

These tests will help you to discover if the child is 'all right-sided' or 'all left-sided', either of which is normal. A mixture can be a factor in the jigsaw pattern of why a child presents us with these difficulties, so if a child is undecided about which hand or eye or foot to use, make a note of it.

Five simple *tests* to give a guide to *laterality*.

Hand

1   Ask the child to write his name or draw a picture on a large piece of paper.

Do not hurry the child.

a) Does he pick up the pencil from the table with his right hand or his left hand?

b) Does he write with his right hand or left hand?

Hand/Eye

2 Use a kaleidoscope or roll up a sheet of paper to look like a telescope. Ask the child to take it from you and look through it.

    a) Does he take it with his right hand or left hand? (This checks the results of Test 1.)

    b) Does he look through the telescope with his right or left eye?

3 Hold the kaleidoscope or the paper telescope upright on the table and ask the child to stand and peer down it with one eye as if it were a microscope.

    a) Does he use his right or left eye? (This checks Test 2b.)

Foot

4 Place a large soft ball, or a ball of loosely crumpled newspaper, well away in front of the child and ask him to run and kick it.

    a) Does he use his right leg and foot or left leg and foot to kick with?

5 Ask the child to hop around the room or outside.

    a) Is the foot on the ground the same foot that kicked the ball? (This checks up on Test 4.)

Use Exercise Sheet 6 for Pointer 6.   Page 81

An original attempt at figures by a child aged 8 years 6 months, and again almost a year later after careful help. His drawings can be seen on page 25.

I am nin. I yoost to doow this buck to font.

SECTION C

Preliminary Exercises

Warming up to Whole Body Movement.

Choose two or three of these to get both you and the child into the 'movement' mood. These are followed by the specific exercises to be selected from Exercise Sheets 1 to 6 corresponding to Pointers 1 to 6, and tailored to the child's particular areas of difficulty already pinpointed as you work through Pointers 1 to 6.

USE OF IMAGINATION

For all children it is important to engage and hold their attention through the imagination. This can be done by introducing each exercise with a lively and familiar image. Several exercises include suggestions for appropriate images, but any others that appeal to the helper or are suggested by the children can be used. The same applies to rhymes, as long as they fit the rhythm.

EXERCISES OUTLINED

Start with the first exercise, for warming up, and work gradually, building up into a whole series. Allow 15-20 minutes for each session. Alternatively, when the child is used to doing the initial exercises, the session can start with one of the more advanced ones, and continue as far as the helper chooses. The bean bag exercises (Exercise Sheet 3) should be performed in sequence as numbered. So if a child should ask to do a particular exercise (and some are more popular than others) see that it is included in its correct position in the series. Some children may find the more complex exercises difficult. The helper will have to decide whether to aid the limbs through the movements or start by holding the child's hands to march in step with the child so that intrinsic feedback can accelerate learning; clearly the child must never be allowed to be just a passive figure.

Whole body

Stand tall, hands by sides, feet slightly apart. Flop forwards from waist, arms dangling loosely. Slowly come up to standing position, arms loosely by sides. Shoulders comfortably back and head level so that eyes look straight ahead.

Hands

Stand or sit. Shake both hands increasingly vigorously in flicking motion from the wrists.

Shoulders

Stand or sit upright on firm chair. Roll shoulders slowly and gently, upwards, and round backwards, dropping down to normal position. Repeat slowly several times.

Head

Stand or sit upright on firm chair. Roll head slowly around and around dropping it forward, chin on chest, round to one side, roll back, over to opposite side, and round to forward position with chin on chest. Repeat several times slowly. (Neck noises, like tiny clicks, are frequently present and only indicate that gentle loosening-up exercises are badly required.)

Breath control

Stand or sit upright. Hands on upper waist (feel the bottom of the rib cage). Deep, slow *breath* in through the nose. Hold for a moment. Open the mouth and let air out steadily. Repeat once or twice (not too much otherwise all the oxygen intake may make you feel quite giddy).

Voice

Deep slow breath in, and hum 'mmm' on one continuous note, with outgoing breath, making sure the sound resonates. If correctly produced, the humming 'mmm' should have both lips tingling with vibration and the sinuses echoing the sound evenly.

Learning to Listen.

This helps everything and everyone so much; very few young children do really listen, although their hearing is normal. This is something they need to learn.

Age to start: 3-4 years, but it is never too late to begin this sort of exercise or to go back and repeat as needed.

Ears

1   Child shuts eyes; listens to each sound and guesses what it is. For example:

- A watch ticking.

- A tap running.

- A pencil tapping on a hard surface.

- A box of matches being rattled.

- A bunch of keys being jangled.

- Fingers clicking.

- Hand clap (one).

Add other simple but clear sounds and continue them for a few minutes every day until you are sure that the child is really listening and of course concentrating too.

2   Open a window or front door. Stand with the child and ask him what he can hear.

3   When out in the garden or park, ask the child to tell you what he hears, even tiny sounds, perhaps a grasshopper, a dragon fly or a honey bee.

4   Ask the child to make some noises with different objects (wooden spoon on saucepan, squeaker toy, opening a door) and you guess what the sound is. Make it a varied fun game with a very particular purpose: listening practice.

Eyes

Just as listening needs practice, so does learning to listen and look at the same time. Ask the child to locate a certain sound (perhaps a house fly) which is not immediately visible, then go and find it to tell you where the sound can be seen.

**Listening to Speech Sounds with
Speech Sounds Explained.**

From listening to a variety of different sounds, move on to listening to speech sounds. The child can have his eyes wide open and watch your lips as well as listen (usual visual and auditory channels). Sometimes try with his back turned or eyes shut, so that he just uses his ears to listen. Using a mirror for the child to watch you and himself to make the sounds can help too.

The following diagram and chart show details of speech organs and phonic sounds.

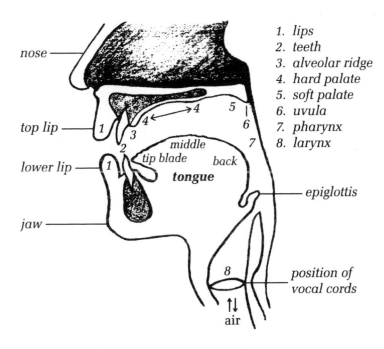

1. *lips*
2. *teeth*
3. *alveolar ridge*
4. *hard palate*
5. *soft palate*
6. *uvula*
7. *pharynx*
8. *larynx*

Diagram showing main organs of speech.

Sound Category	Voiceless	Voiced	Sound Creation
Plosives	p	b	*Lips together, briefly.*
	t	d	*Tongue tip on alveolar ridge, briefly.*
	c, k	g	*Back of tongue against soft palate, briefly.*
Fricatives	f	v	*Top teeth lightly on bottom lip.*
	th	th	*Tongue tip between teeth, gently.*
	s	z	*Tongue and alveolar ridge close, teeth very close.*
	sh	sh	*Tongue edges and upper side teeth very close.*
	h		*Open mouth and blow.*
Affricates	ch	j	*Tongue against alveolar ridge, slow release.*
Lateral Non-fricative		l	*Tongue tip touching centre of alveolar ridge.*
Semi-vowels		w	*Rounded lips.*
		y	*Mouth slightly open, lips back.*
Frictionless Continuant		r	*Tongue tip raised behind alveolar ridge, not touching it.*
Nasal		m	*Lips together, hold. Sound down nose.*
		n	*Tongue tip up, hold. Sound down nose.*
		ng	*Back of tongue up, hold. Sound down nose.*
Vowels	Pure short:		/a/ /e/ /i/ /o/ /u/ /oo/ /er/
	long:		/ee/ /ah/ /aw/ /oo/ /er/
	Diphthongs:		/ay/ /oh/ /I/ /ow/ /oi/ /eer/ /air/ /ure/ /ew/
	Triphthongs:		/ire/ /our/

All vowels are voiced, and each word has at least one in it.

Chart showing categories of phonic sounds.

Sound Steps to Link into Words.

Some children find it very difficult or even impossible to make certain single consonant sounds which should normally be mastered easily by the end of Infant School or 7 years of age. By then the more formal story writing and spelling work introduced at school will become increasingly hard for the child if the link between clear speech sounds and auditory (heard) perception has not been fully established.

Single consonants build into *consonant blends* or consonants linked together. Here are some examples of double consonants at the beginning or end of single words:

	In blends:	*and word ends:*
ch	chair	match
sh	shoe	mash
th	thin, there	moth
wh	why and nowhere, everywhere!	

Because so many children aged much over 7 years of age still pronounce the blend /th/ as a /f/ or /v/ and have difficulty spelling words that sound the same to them, for example, 'fin/thin', or 'for/thaw', a special sound step workbook for discrimination practice between /f/, /v/ and /th/ may be needed.

Some double consonant blends with a single word example are shown overleaf.

Vowel sounds are sometimes hard to make clearly; use the mirror to let the child see the changing shape of your open mouth. Start very simply with the five short vowel sounds a, e, i, o and u.

a	apple	e	egg
i	it	o	on
u	under		

Try singing the vowel sounds aloud.

pl	(please)	**Plese**	pr	(pretty)	**Prite**
bl	(blue)	**Blow**	br	(bruise)	**Bros**
tr	(tree)	**tree**	tw	(twenty)	**tente**
dr	(drink)	**drink**	dw	(dwell)	**drwel**
cl	(clap)	**cap**	cr	(cream)	**crem**
kw	– always written qu (queen)				
gl	(glue)	**glow**	gr	(green)	**green**
sp	(spot)	**sot**	st	(stop)	**shop**
sc	(scum)	**6omn**	sk	(skip)	**sip**
sm	(smoke)	**sok**	sn	(snag)	**sig**
sl	(slip)	**sitp**	sw	(swing)	**sinim swinq**
fl	(flower)	**flower**	fr	(frog)	**frog**

The illustrations above are examples of double consonant blends not fully established in spelling of an intelligent boy aged 9 years 9 months. Hearing test result: normal. Note: /s/ blends are greatest group of difficulty.

Triple consonant blends build words together:

spl	(splash)	str	(string)
spr	(spring)	squ	(squirrel)
thr	(three – not 'free')		

Build single words into sentences aloud. Ask the child to make up a sentence for a given word and say it to you aloud.

Write words down, let the child look at them and copy underneath if he wants to.

Draw pictures of groups of words with the same blend. Ask the child to put a name to the picture and colour it in.

Build from the recognition of the spoken sound to recognition of the associated written symbol.

Use lots of variety of approach and introduce games. Here are a few examples:

Nonsense sequences: Say aloud three or four nonsense sounds:

    p-t-l   g-w-p-b

    f-m-d   g-m-f-sh

Ask the child to repeat exactly each nonsense sequence after you. Let him make up some for you to copy aloud.

I-Spy: use the name as well as the initial sound.

Rhyming: build upon nursery rhymes, simple poems and catchy tunes with words. Find simple words which rhyme aloud:

    top:mop   ring:sing

    rope:soap   rumble:tumble

Then make up a rhyming sentence or verse using the words to build around with more words. Make it fun, make it snappy! The co-author's book *Phonic Rhyme Time* (also available through The Robinswood Press) may be useful for further explanation and practice of speech sounds and rhymes.

The man is jumping over a fense.

The cat is on the wall.

The dog has found his bone.

K.L.S. Age 12.5

This pupil, aged 12 years 6 months, has severe sequencing difficulties, and is showing here that she can see, with picture clues, the linking verbs that separate the nouns.

SECTION D

Exercise Sheets

EXERCISE SHEET 1 for POINTER 1.
Timing and Rhythm.

TIMING

Sit facing the child, both of you sitting comfortably. He may watch as well as listen. Each action must be copied exactly by the child.

('---' indicates a pause)

One clap
Two quick claps
One stamp with foot
Two stamps with one foot and two with the other.

Clap --- clap, clap
Clap, clap --- clap
Clap, clap, clap --- clap.

When variations with three or four claps are exhausted, mix in some foot tapping.

Tap, tap (with one foot)
Tap --- tap, tap (with one foot).

Build up to a variety of up to six taps or claps. This is a simple programme:

Clap --- clap, clap --- clap, clap
Tap, tap (other foot now) tap, tap, tap
Clap, clap, clap --- tap, tap, tap.

Continue this clapping and tapping programme in various sequences until the child's actions echo your own with really snappy accuracy.

Ask the child to make up a clap, tap or mixed sequence for you to copy. It is often very hard for the child to create the idea himself. Help him by taking turns until he improves and is as good as you.

RHYTHM

Rhythm exercises are fun when played as a guessing game. Think of a nursery rhyme and clap the rhythm. The child has to guess which one it is.

Then ask the child to choose a well known nursery rhyme and clap it out. You guess. If you can't because the child is so bad at it, have a laugh ('silly me' attitude, do not blame the child). When you find out which rhyme he was trying, clap it out together, singing the tune as you go. Alternatively, you can start by singing the rhyme and clapping together, then go on to the guessing game.

Once singing and clapping in time have been achieved the child uses whole body movements to:

> March around the room with a really good swing of the arms and an even stride of legs in proper time to your steady cheerful beat on a tambourine, triangle or drum, or even to your brisk hand clapping. Break into applause at the end of the performance.

Your encouragement and mutual enjoyment are vital to success.

The child chooses a nursery rhyme and walks it out around the room using his whole body to get across the rhythm of his chosen rhyme to you. Practise together once or twice to get the idea before the guessing game begins.

For older children

Allow the child to give a pictorial image of words wherever possible.

Use pictures and make a list in good clear handwriting of words which the child finds difficult to say accurately.

Say each word in syllables for him – e.g. caravan. Clap it, walk it: then keeping to the natural rhythm, spell it out aloud.

Thus the child will see it written down, hear it said very distinctly in syllables, clap and walk it in rhythm, then spell it out aloud, and finally say the word again, with a feel for the rhythm.

Examples of suitable poems

- for rhythm and colour:

The Rainbow

Red and orange and yellow and green,
The rainbow's colours have a bright shiny sheen;
Light blue and indigo and violet all told,
At the end of the rainbow is a pot of gold.

- for rhythm and imagination:

The Fairies (William Allingham)

Up the airy mountain
Down the rushy glen,
We daren't go a-hunting
For fear of little men;
Wee folk, good folk,
Trooping all together;
Green jacket, red cap,
And White Owl's feather!

EXERCISE SHEET 2 for POINTER 2.
Direction.

General Exercises.

POINTING

The child stands comfortably, arms down. Practise giving orders for him to follow. He should repeat the orders aloud and carry them out.

- "Point up" (straight up, not vaguely at an angle).

- "Point down" (directly down to the floor).

- "Point in front" (again, make sure it is in front, or half to the side).

- "Point behind."

Point to the door, window, light and other objects in the room. Then, with eyes closed, take it in turns to say "Point to ..." Open eyes and see how close you are. Repeat daily until exercise becomes too easy.

STEPPING

Both feet together:

- Forward: "One step forward."

- Backward: "One step back."

- Sideways: "One step sideways" (either way).

- Left: "One step to the left."

- Right: "One step to the right."

Give the child a chance to give orders as well, and make sure he really understands and uses words like 'above', 'behind', 'below', 'underneath', 'wide', 'turn', 'bend', then on to 'turn around' and 'bend down'.

JUMPING

Younger children

Stand with feet together, hands down. Learn to jump forwards: still facing forwards, jump sideways, forwards and backwards to given orders.

Age 9 upwards

Jump on the spot:

- to the side (exact 90° angle from forward position), to the back (90° turn),

- to the other side (90° turn),

- to the front (90° turn).

The child should now be in the original position. Try doing this exercise together. It is hard to stay balanced on the spot after each jump has been accurately performed.

MULTIPLE INSTRUCTIONS

If several instructions are given at once, the child may be confused and never reach his destination. Help him by using these exercises – they can be played as a soldier game. Ask him to repeat orders aloud after you, then carry them out. Examples:

- "Stand up, take one step forward." (Two part command.)

- "Sit down, one arm up." (Two part command.)

- "Stand up. Take one step back, then two to the left." (Three part command.)

As the child progresses, add to the commands:

- "Take one step to the left, three steps back, four to the right and six forward."

Compass

Work out with the child the position of North, South, East and West on a paper drawing. Then tell him in which direction he is facing: in the room, at the front of the house, the back, into the garden out of the bedroom window and from the kitchen.

Use a compass if possible for further directional practice. Aim to get the child to see beyond his immediate environment to the distant church spire, hills or other landmarks.

Outings

When setting out for a walk, tell the child in advance where to turn – e.g. post box or friend's house – and in which direction. Let him walk in front and lead the way but do not, of course, tell him the destination. By following your directions he will discover where he is to end the adventure.

Above/below awareness

The child stands still and steady, feet together, hands by sides. Get him to rise very slowly on to his toes, hold for a few seconds, then come very slowly down. He must feel himself rise up higher and come down lower, saying the words that explain the movement as he does it.

DIRECTION ON SELF (Body Geography)

Make sure that the child knows the names of the various parts of the body. Many confusions over the position of ankles and shoulders, eyebrows and waist occur.

Horizontally

The child lies down on his back on the floor. He repeats each command before carrying it out:

- "Raise one arm." (Say "down again" after each command.)
- "Raise one leg."
- "Raise head."
- "Raise left arm."
- "Raise right leg."
- "Raise right arm and left leg."
- "Raise head."
- "Raise shoulders."
- "Raise knees."

Continue and vary the orders as required.

This exercise can advance to:

1 The child's eyes being lightly closed whilst carrying out commands as above.
2 The child lying on his front and working out commands from that position.

Vertically

The child sits or stands; ask him to touch his:

nose	ankles
left ear	chin
back of neck	cheeks
right foot	waist
tummy	hips
shoulders	elbows

Repeat this exercise with the child's eyes lightly closed.

Let the child stand facing you. With his eyes shut ask him to touch your:

nose	hair
chin	ear
left hand	right hand

Outline

Ask the child to stand against a suitable wall (covered in brown paper or newspaper if necessary) and you draw around his outline shape with a thick crayon or chalk.

The child is asked to step away and look at his image, then draw in the parts of the body, naming them aloud as he works, drawing in clothing and other items, e.g. wristwatch, on the correct wrist.

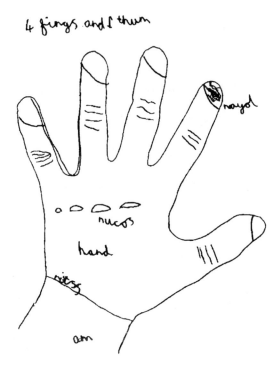

Example of an 8 year old's own left hand image and his labels for the parts.

Link up with Exercise Sheet 5 for Pointer 5.   Page 65

47

EXERCISE SHEET 3 for POINTER 3.
Spatial Orientation and Movement.

A Series of 8 Specific Exercises with a Bean Bag.

These exercises stimulate awareness of space around the body and encourage understanding of orientation in space. The instructions specify either right or left hand to begin the exercise, but the individual child should be encouraged to commence with his or her 'writing hand'.

Comments: Once an exercise has been mastered to some degree, the difficulty of maintaining a steady rhythm may remain. The teacher could then use a tambourine, triangle or drum, with or without a poem. In the case of younger children, i.e. under 6 years, a very familiar nursery rhyme should be said in unison with the teacher. For instance, a rhyme to go with exercise 1 for the younger children would be:

Jack and Jill went up the hill.

They would then throw the bean bag on the beat – as under-lined – that is four throws to a line.

A more complicated rhythm is better fun for older children, e.g.

This old man, he played one
He played nick nack on his drum
With a nick nack paddy whack, Give a dog a bone
This old man came rolling home.

Rhythm marks (not beat marks) are underlined. Rhythms can vary, beats do not.

All exercises unless specified to the contrary start with the children standing upright, feet together, arms at side.

Exercise 1 – Giving and Receiving.

Throwing the bean bag from one hand and catching it in the other. The teacher could suggest that the bean bag is something precious so that the child learns to receive it gently with open, relaxed hand rather than grabbing it. The child becomes aware of movement from one side of the body to the other. The exercise encourages the ability, often lacking, of the hand to turn from palm up to palm down. When done quietly, the sound of the beans in the bag is quite audible. This should encourage listening and concentration. A silent rhythm could be done such as an anapaest – two short throws then on the long throw the bean bag could be passed behind the back to the other hand.

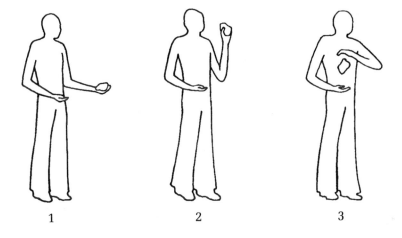

1   2   3

1 Stand straight, hands at wrist level palms upward, bean bag on left palm.

2 Raise left hand, gradually turning it over, elbow coming away from waist.

3 Left elbow pushed out from waist, left palm downwards, bean bag drops into right palm, right hand gives a little under weight of bean bag.

To complete the circuit, follow the same procedure dropping the bean bag from the right hand back to the left.

Full Exercise: Repeat the exercise several times, keeping a careful rhythm throughout.

The exercise can also be done sitting, and with hands at shoulder level. It can be combined with walking, running, hopping, skipping. In this case the bean bag should be received into the hand to match the leading leg.

The exercise can be done to a poem. If so, the younger children should throw the bag on the beat, and the older children should throw it on each syllable. Once mastered, the exercise can be done to a drum or tambourine – or may be done silently.

Exercise 2 – Making a Ring Around the Waist.

This helps the child by defining his own centre and peripheral space, and so encourages awareness of his position in space.

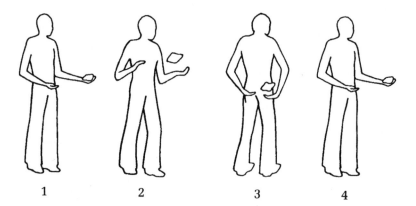

| 1 | 2 | 3 | 4 |

1 Starting position.

2 Stand hands in front at waist level, palms upwards, bean bag in left hand, throw bean bag from left to right hand.

3 Bean bag in right hand, move both hands behind back. Throw bean bag from right to left hand.

4   Bring arms back to starting position.

Continue passing the bean bag around in a ring, in a clockwise direction.

Full Exercise: Repeat 1-4, five times.

- The whole movement should describe a ring about the waist.

- Hands to be kept as near to waist level as possible, elbows flexed.

- Reach out behind as far as possible before throwing.

Exercise 3 – The Rainbow.

This encourages awareness of space over one's head. At first, in movement No. 2 (see illustrations page 52), the children may need to pass the bean bag rather than throw it. When they start throwing it they will probably first need to watch the bean bag travelling overhead. With practice the child should be able to look straight ahead. To foster the child's awareness of the space above his head, the teacher could usefully suggest that the movement of the arms and bag describes a rainbow, with the child standing underneath.

1   Stand, arms held out sideways, palms upwards, bean bag in right hand.

2   Bring both arms upwards, palms facing each other, pass or throw bean bag from right to left hand.

3   Bean bag now in left hand, bring both arms down to position 1.

4   Bring both arms upwards again, palms facing each other, pass or throw bean bag from left to right hand.

5   Bean bag now in right hand, bring both arms down again to position 1.

Full Exercise: Repeat 1-5, eight times.

1

2

3

4

5

Key Factor: With practice it will be possible to throw bean bag over increasing space looking straight ahead and catching it successfully.

Exercise 4 – Throwing Bean Bag over the Shoulder.

This exercise encourages awareness of space around one's back. The teacher could suggest the image of water falling down one's back.

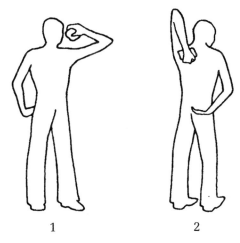

1   2

1 Left hand holds bean bag over left shoulder, right hand behind back at hip level, palm upwards.

2 Drop bean bag from left to right hand.

A whole sequence includes:

3 Bean bag in right hand, right hand holds bean bag over right shoulder, left hand behind back at hip level, palm upwards.

4 Drop bean bag from right to left hand.

Full Exercise: Repeat sequence eight times.

Exercise 5 – Under and Over.

This is the first of the exercises to include the lower limbs, to encourage awareness of them, and co-ordinate them with the arms. The exercise reinforces lateral awareness.

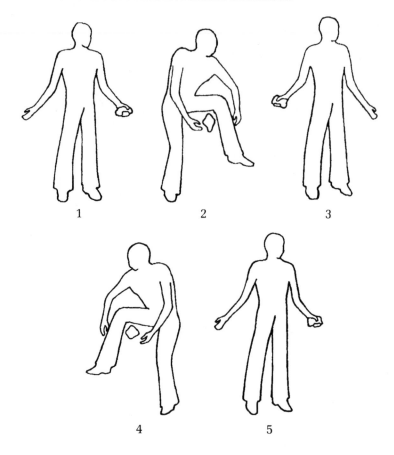

1 Arms sideways, hands at waist level, palms upwards, bean bag in left hand.

2 Raise left leg, knee flexed, pass bean bag under left leg, from left to right hand.

3 Bean bag now in right hand, left leg down.

4 Raise right leg, knee flexed, pass bean bag under right leg, from right to left hand.

5 Bean bag now in left hand, right leg down.

For a later faster variation, try throwing the bean bag rather than passing it, while hopping with the legs.

Full Exercise: Repeat 1-5, in one continuous movement, eight times.

Key Factor: Awareness of a figure 8 on its side.

Exercise 6 – Foot Exercises with Bean Bag.

This exercise stimulates tactile awareness through the use of the child's feet, of balance, pressure, temperature and texture. It uses the muscles of the feet and toes and includes direction-finding away from the child's centre.

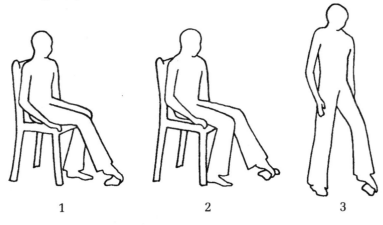

1   2   3

1 Sit, straight back, bean bag on floor in front of right foot, curl toes around bean bag to pick it up, lift it and drop it.

2 Sit, straight back, bean bag on floor in front of left foot, curl toes around bean bag to pick it up, lift it and drop it.

3 Repeat 1 and 2 standing.

Full Exercise: Repeat 1 - 2 standing and sitting until grasping and lifting are easy.

Repeat 1 - 2 throwing bean bag backwards, forwards, left, right.

Key Factor: To be done with *bare feet.*

Exercise 7 – Standing Figure of '8' (Eight).

This encourages awareness of space around the body and incorporates the diagonal direction.

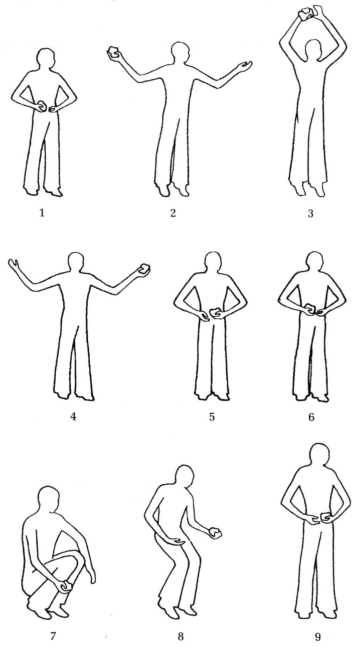

1 Hands close together at centre point, bean bag in right hand.

2 Both arms curve sideways and upwards, at the same time rise on toes.

3 On toes, arms overhead, pass bean bag from right to left hand.

1 - 3

4 Bean bag now in left hand, both arms return sideways, also lower heels.

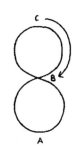

5 Hands together at centre point palms upwards, bean bag in left hand, feet together flat on floor.

6 Pass bean bag from left to right hand.

3 - 6

7 Bean bag in right hand, both arms curve downwards and sideways, crouch with straight back, pass bean bag under knees from right to left hand.

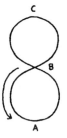

6 - 7

8 Bean bag now in left hand, rise to standing position, arms curving sideways and upwards back to centre point (9).

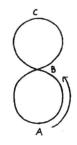

Full Exercise: Repeat 1-9, eight times.

8 - 9

Diagram of movement.

Variation: Two people stand facing each other, one holds a bean bag in his right hand. This is thrown to the other's right right hand which he then passes around his back to his left hand. He then throws it back to the other's left hand. The first person passes the bean bag behind his back. They are now in the starting position having created a horizontal figure eight around them.

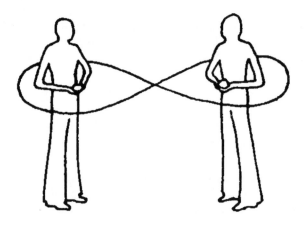

Exercise 8 – Spiral.

This exercise incorporates all directions in space taken separately in previous exercises – up, down, right, left, in, out. It begins as a large spiral narrowing as it rises, then on the descent it widens as it falls, in one rhythmic flow.

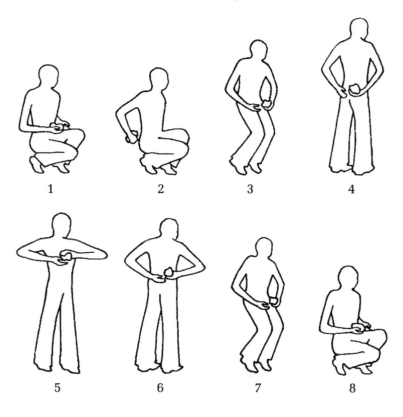

1   Crouch on toes, straight back, hands front at waist level, palms upwards, bean bag in right hand.

2   Hands behind back, pass bean bag from right to left hand.

3   Rise to half crouch still on toes, hands return to front at hip level, pass bean bag from left to right hand.

4   Standing hands behind back, pass bean bag from right to left hand.

5 Standing hands in front, shoulder level, elbows out, pass bean bag from left to right hand.

6 Standing hands behind back, pass bean bag from right to left hand – *above waist level.*

7 Half crouch on toes, hands return front at hip level, pass bean bag from left to right hand.

8 Crouch on toes, straight back, hands behind back, pass bean bag from right to left hand, return to Number 1.

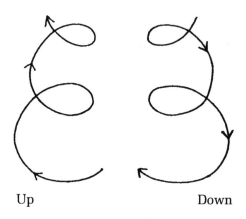

Up   Down

Diagram of movement.

Note that the bean bag spirals in one *direction* only in one rhythmic flow.

Full Exercise: Repeat 1-8, eight times.

Key Factor: This exercise must be done with a straight back.

EXERCISE SHEET 4 for POINTER 4.
Sequencing.

A few minutes practice every day will help a child to follow a proper sequence.

FOR THE YOUNG CHILD 3-7 YEARS

Beads

Threading beads by colour alternately – one red, one blue and so on. Then on to three colours. Build up a sequence of three red, two blue, one white.

Buttons

Sorting buttons into a long line by sizes with the smallest at one end increasing to the biggest at the other.

Bows

Tying shoe laces or knotting a tie calls for endless patience and constant practice. The child should follow your instructions, spoken quietly in a rhythm. "Up and over, under and through" or whatever you feel is appropriate. When the task is satisfactorily complete, say "well done". Avoid an impatient "I'll do it for you because you're too slow".

7 YEARS UPWARDS

Calendar

Let the child help you make a calendar. This can be done in easy stages spread over several weeks:

Days of the week. First, cut out seven equal sized pieces of cardboard for the days of the week. Write a day on each and say them aloud. Lay them on the table in order, say them aloud again, getting the child to join in and find the rhythm of the days.

Months of the year. Next cut out twelve larger, equal sized pieces of cardboard for the months of the year. Follow the same procedure as for the days of the week, writing them down, saying them aloud, setting them out in the right order.

Dates and seasons. Then cut out thirty-one discs, numbering them for the dates of the month, and finally four squares, one for each season of the year.

On a large cardboard sheet, which the child can colour brightly, set out four big blobs of Blue-tack or similar adhesive. The child selects the relevant pieces according to what day, date, month and season it is, and sticks them up on the calendar daily for everyone to admire. A home-made calendar may not be perfect, but to the child it is much more meaningful than one bought in the shop.

Alphabet

Help the child to *learn* the alphabet in rhythmic sections. First with pauses as marked (or as the school teacher recommends):

ABC/DEF/GHI/JKL/MNO/PQR/STU/VW/XYZ

Then build up to:

ABCDEFG/HIJKLMN/OPQRSTU/VWXYZ

and progress to managing the alphabet aloud steadily all the way through.

Alphabet game. Ask the child to listen to make sure you say the alphabet 'properly' and have not left out a letter in any group. He will have great fun telling you to 'stop' where he hears a mistake.

Alphabet game. The child stands in a clear space, and from that point walks the shape of one letter of the alphabet on the floor, starting at the point where we write from on paper.

Use the lower case (small) letters, not upper case (capital) letters.

Practise one or two each day. Once the child can manage the letter shape in space, using the whole body, he is less likely to reverse it on paper.

Single letter set. Acquire an alphabet of good sized wooden (or plastic) letters, or make your own by drawing clear crayon or felt tip lettering on 2 same size cards (all capital letters or all small letters, do not mix both). The child arranges them in order around himself in a semi-circle. He practises looking, saying aloud, pointing out the ones that are missing. Finding and naming letters that are hidden around the room can be fun, tracing the feel of the letter with fingers together helps build tactile sense.

Touch alphabet. 'Draw' letter shapes, one at a time, on the child's back and ask him to guess which they are, no looking allowed and no sound made. He will enjoy 'drawing' letters on another willing child's back or on yours. This can be a lot of fun and gives excellent sensory image practice as well as building up awareness of touch shape. Numbers can be 'drawn' in this way too, not mixed with touch alphabet, but as a separate exercise.

Alphabet tracking. Find a page of clear printed story (as in the Ladybird Book Series) and ask the child to take a pencil and *circle* around the first 'a' letter he comes to, then find and circle the first 'b' letter which appears after the 'a', keeping the sequence of the alphabet going down the page, with the eyes running left to right along each line, not jumping about but building up visual tracking and alphabet skill in the word form.

stil on a p cred myf b ix mo c hez togu
jo d h e lk pyx wrog ilz vu f smolt nik
truz g amp h yb tawp vox sanc quork
fyrz tuc k i e ba j paz wren k tux daf
wabs hu l t m y ga n d tev b o cer fatz
ge p y bast q uack gax sich r baf biz
jalf deb s e t ch gok chay h u ken mib
nep bafil v b chone ply a w ec grik
cro x ah strel y be me z quelp noch

Example of alphabet tracking using specially designed nonsense words, with easy left to right tracking sequence; from part of the *Ann Arbor Tracking Program.*

Numbers sequencing

Each number from 1-9 has a different shape which the child may have trouble in recalling on to paper in the right direction or shape. It can help considerably to work out the numbers by using the body to step out the imaginary shape on the floor. The child's feet must step out the movement that the hand and pencil would normally attempt, starting at the top of the number, never from the bottom upwards.

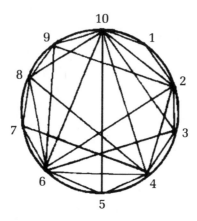

Times Tables. Place ten equal markers in a circle on the floor, leaving room for a child's step between each marker. Ask the child to walk from marker 1 to marker 2, 3, 4 up to 10 in ten steps. Build up ability by asking the child to walk from marker 1 to 3, then 3 to 5, then 5 to 7 and 7 to 9. The variations are considerable and can be continued as required.

The child walks round the ten markers in ten steps. Then he says the times tables as he goes: for 2 x tables he starts at point 2, says 2 x 1 = 2, goes on to point 4 saying 2 x 2 = 4, and on to point 6 saying, 2 x 3 = 6. By 2 x 6 he will be at point 2 again. With this whole body rhythm method, use the large-type (easy to see, easy to say) Old Fashioned Times Table Book published by Ward Lock Educational.

Link up with Exercise Sheet 5 for Pointer 5,
Writing Exercises.   Page 69

EXERCISE SHEET 5 for POINTER 5.
Fine Motor Control for Speech, Writing and Reading.

SPEECH EXERCISES

The child who occasionally dribbles and gulps more than other children should:

CHEWING

Practise *chewing* exercises: Orbit sugar-less chewing gum, bubble gum (big bubbles, no troubles) or, if you disapprove, nothing in the mouth at all, with lips together firmly and consciously. Use a mirror for the child to watch himself and your mouth for comparison.

SWALLOWING

After a few chews comes a *swallow* with lips firmly together. Have a star ready to reward success and stick it on the mirror.

JAW/LIPS

In front of a mirror, practise 'mouth closed' count up to ten whilst holding closure. Then let him relax. Increase counting and therefore lip closure times as the days go by. A conscious effort on the part of the child need not be forced if triumph is in the air.

BREATHING

The child who persistently breathes through the mouth needs to practise breathing through his *nose* with lips closed, in a conscious attempt at control. Build up a rhythm: air in through the nose and out through the mouth.

NOSE BLOWING

Practise *blowing* his nose correctly with a tissue (breath in quickly through open mouth, shut it up fast, and puff down nose).

MOUTH

After cleaning the teeth the child must really swill cool water around his entire mouth, into his cheeks, then spit it out strongly into the basin; this action really makes the muscles work and tones up movement.

TONGUE

Tongue exercises for sluggish movers:

Stick right out; stretch the tongue right out as hard as possible, then relax. Now try putting tongue out and

- Up towards nose.

- Down to chin.

- Out to one cheek.

- Then over to other.

Have a game with 'Mr Tongue'. Make a story: Can he see along the road? Now along the road the other way. Is the sky blue today? (up towards nose). Down for a look to see if any puddles are on the pavement (down towards chin). Move tongue rapidly, flip it in and out, making a Red Indian noise as it goes realistically into action.

BLOWING

Blowing is the opposite of *sucking* and both must be in good order for speech, and incidentally, a healthy person.

Practise:

- Puffing out cheeks.

- Sucking in cheeks to make hollows.

- Blowing bubbles through straw dipped in bowl of water.

- Sucking up pieces of torn up paper with a straw.

- Blowing a ping pong ball along a table top; try with a straw, directing the stream of air and controlling the ping pong ball towards a 'goal'.

Speech defects will only improve if the organs needed to create speech are in good working order. If the above exercises are put into full swing then clear speech should be possible. Your local Health Centre or Hospital based Speech and Language Therapist is there to advise you about all speech and language difficulties. She (or he) will visit you at home if you cannot reach a Centre, so do not put off contact because of travelling costs or transport problems.

Speech problems which 'hardly notice', or words that are 'nearly right', deserve a closer listen. Make a list of longer words that are often troublesome when said out aloud. Sometimes the child will change the longer word for a shorter 'easier' one. Some words are close but not quite right. Examples:

Chimney	Often said as: chim/ber/ley
Probably	Often said as: prob/erly or prob/ly
Scrambled	Has been heard as 'strangled'. Imagine 'strangled' eggs for breakfast!
Breakfast	Breakfast is hard to spell when thought of and said as breff/first or 'first-breff-of-a-day'.
Vegetable	Veger/bles or just 'ugh'.
Badminton	Dab/it/on.
Especially	Speciality.
Bald/bold/boiled	A 'bald' egg for tea makes sense to a child...

Whenever you notice that your child has trouble with a word, write it down so that it can be included in the exercise list. Let the child hear the word said clearly and written down; break the word into syllables both aloud and on paper. Let the child repeat aloud after you; never laugh at the difficulty experienced trying to say the word correctly; always encourage successful attempts, and stop once achieved; don't ask for repeat performances. Let it come naturally by reinforcing the practice again next day, trying the difficult word in a sentence, seeing if it stays 'right' or if it reverts back to the old way. Build from establishing a word in isolation to correct use in a sentence and then into conversation.

As you work you will begin to realise that maybe the child's own understanding of words is actually weaker than you thought. Many words sound alike to the child, so 'how' is 'who', and 'are' is 'our'. Many examples appear that you will find easy enough (s'nuff?) without mentioning 'lemon mangled pie' (the lemon has to be mangled in the squeezer, does it not?). So what is 'meringue' to do with it? Well, that's a completely different language!

DIET

Catarrhal problems can be made worse by eating too much dairy produce, cheese, milk and eggs. It is worth trying a few weeks of pure fruit juice (not orange with added colour) instead of milk, sticks of raw carrot and celery plus apples and natural foods, including wholemeal bread, avoiding additives, artificial colouring or dyes. These can easily be spotted on food labelling as 'E' numbers, part of the standard European codes in the UK.

Dietary plans as part of an overall educational programme are proving most beneficial for some children with specified learning difficulties, helping to regulate behaviour patterns and improve concentration span.

Link up with Section E for Further Reading.   Page 96

WRITING EXERCISES

Writing exercises are useless unless the fingers which hold the pen are moving very finely indeed. Even before the fingers, the hands have to co-ordinate, together with the eyes. All must work smoothly to produce neat easy-to-read handwriting.

FINGERS AND THUMBS

Finger exercises

1 Choose either the left hand or right hand first. With left hand, rotate thumb clockwise; with right hand, rotate thumb anti-clockwise, around first finger, then second, third and fourth, then back again round third, second and finally the first finger. Repeat exactly in correct direction with each hand. This exercise needs practice and patience to get fingers really under control.

2 One hand at a time, then later both together, call out to the child with orders for "thumb to touch second finger", "thumb to touch fourth finger", etc.

3 The child places his hands together as for praying. Ask him to turn in: thumbs, first fingers, second fingers, third fingers (hardest), fourth fingers. Straighten between each action.

4 Take each hand in turn and tell the child to wriggle the individual finger (first to fourth) or thumbs. It is almost impossible to wriggle the second (middle) finger without the third joining in a bit.

HANDS

Hand co-ordinating exercises

1 Place both hands on the table, palms down. Turn the left hand over. Now switch over, left hand turning palm down, right hand coming palm up. Switch over again and again slowly increasing speed until rhythm breaks down and hands fail to co-ordinate exactly.

2 Place both hands on table. Clench left fist, right hand outstretched. Swap clenching and outstretched hands over and over again, building up rhythm and pace, until sequence breaks.

Hand control and finger mobility exercises.

Use a soft ball or orange held in the palm, and against which each finger in turn can be extended then returned. Both hands should have a turn!

1

2

Special Exercise 1 – Wrist and Finger Movements with Rod.

This exercise encourages central conscious control through fluid wrist and finger movement controlling one side of the body, or both simultaneously. It helps to alleviate tension which often builds up in the hand and wrist, especially if the handwriting is cramped. The shoulder and elbow joints should remain relaxed. It can be done to a poem, e.g.:

Mix a pancake, stir a pancake, pop it in the pan.
Fry a pancake, toss a pancake, catch it if you can!

The rod should be at least 43 cms (15"), ideally made of copper – 2cm dowelling would do.

 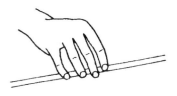

Kneel like this. Hold the rod with little finger away from you. The end of the rod nearest the little finger rests on the floor. The rod starts almost horizontal.

1   Starting position. Rod points to 12 o'clock, i.e. *away* from body, forwards, with palm downwards.

2   Propel rod clockwise till end points to 3 o'clock, palm downwards.

3

4

3   Propel rod with little finger till end points to 6 o'clock, i.e. towards body, palm now faces *inwards* to mid body line.

4   Propel rod till end points to 9 o'clock, at same time rotate wrist to turn palm *upwards*, i.e. fingers now *under* rod, thumb on *top*.

5   Propel rod till rod points back to 12 o'clock. At same time rotate wrist and turn palm *downwards* again.

When achieved successfully kneeling, repeat exercise standing, with rod held straight out in front.

EXERCISE PROGRESSION

With practice, both hands can hold rods and simultaneously describe circles in opposite directions, both circles outward moving.

Full Exercise: Repeat 1-5, eight times with right hand (as printed) and eight times with left.

Key Factor: The rod must be held centrally. Rest it against the thumb, with 4 fingers on it. Propel it in a circular movement clockwise in the right hand, anticlockwise in the left.

Special Exercise 2 – Finger Movements with Rod.

The rod must be held as still as possible, the upper arms remaining at the side of the body, the elbows still. The rhythmic element of this exercise helps the mobility and skill of fingers and wrists. First rhythmic execution is important, and to help achieve it the teacher could say this poem:

Pepper and salt. Pepper and salt.
Under and over with never a fault.

Pep... raise both index fingers simultaneously off rod, then replace fingertips.

...per raise middle fingers off rod, replace fingertips.

and raise ring finger, replace fingertips.

salt raise little fingers, replace fingertips.

1

2

1 Starting position. Rod horizontal at shoulder level, elbows flexed close to body, fingertips on top, thumbs supporting rod.

2 First line of poem. Repeat, starting with index fingers again.

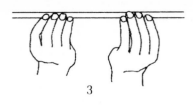

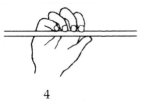

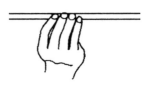

3 Change hand position, rod now rests on fingertips, thumb on top of rod.

4 Change hand position. Fingers, wrist and rod now in starting position.

Second line of poem

Under	Number 3.
and over	Number 4.
with never	Number 3.
a fault	Number 4.

Key Factor: Rod remains at shoulder level throughout exercise.

WRITING POSITION AND PREPARATION

A child cannot produce good writing unless he is seated correctly at a desk or table with the chair at the right height. He should sit upright (do not allow him to crouch over his work), with both feet comfortably on the floor, not one on top of the other or curled round the chair leg. He holds the pencil in a firm but easy grip, with his arm, almost from elbow to wrist, resting on the desk, relaxed and in to his body. The non-writing hand steadies the paper, which should be set straight, not at an angle, in front of him. Triangular pencil grips in cheerful colours are available from LDA (address on page 99). These help stop an incorrectly held pencil becoming a permanent habit.

PRE-WRITING EXERCISE USING WHIRL SHAPE

On a full sized sheet of white cardboard draw firmly using a thick crayon on its side to gain a wide band of colour a 'whirl' shape, as illustrated, as an aid for development of fluent control of shoulder, arm, hand and fingers, with co-ordinated eye movements for those with:

1 Little or no writing.

2 Large, uneven or untidy writing.

3 Tiny, cramped hesitant writing.

Diagram of 'whirl' shape for pre-writing exercise. This is an adaptation of an exercise from Audrey McAllen's book 'The Extra Lesson' (see further reading) and it is essential that the spiral is clockwise.

Pin or stick 'whirl' poster to cardboard or cork backing, or the wall. Providing the seated child finds it comfortable, place upright in front of him for hand touch. He may prefer the 'whirl' placed out flat on the floor. Always ensure that the outer starting edge is at the top left hand side.

- Groups 1 and 2 start at outer edge.

- Group 3 starts at centre point.

Thumb and fingers of writing hand should be placed in easy writing position at starting point, and movement around the 'whirl' should be smooth, steady and accurate. Relax after each exercise is completed; repeat 2-3 times initially, building up to 5-6 times.

Advance to using a thick paint brush for over colouring around the 'whirl' always starting at either the outer or inner point. The hand not in use may be occupied by holding a ball or bean bag.

Use daily until improvement in concentration, movement and co-ordination is achieved and maintained. Advance to large writing patterns using paint or fat crayons.

FORM DRAWING

Drawing forms or large writing patterns can be practised with the emphasis *off* 'writing'. This is a word some children have come to dislike, especially if they are rewarded with results which often seem correct to them, but to others show letters that are reversed, upside down, bad, messy or even not there at all.

Children can have very real trouble in getting going on paper, so start with some simple form drawings, using different colours to make the attempts look interesting.

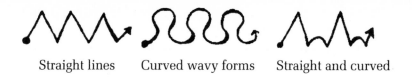

Straight lines	Curved wavy forms	Straight and curved

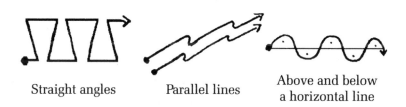

Straight angles	Parallel lines	Above and below a horizontal line

Diagrams of simple form drawings.

The child may try his hand at the numbers 1-10, one big figure to a page, using a fat felt tip pen, a thick soft leaded pencil or a paint brush. Then he can progress to the curved or straight lines which make up the letters of the alphabet, making them big, enjoyable pictures, only one to a page to start with. Keep loose sheets pinned together in sequence to look at again later on.

SPELLING EXERCISES

These exercises are used as an aid and should not be confused with the systematic teaching of spelling in class or by a special educational needs teacher. Let the child sit beside you with his piece of written work, and read it *aloud* to you. Make sure he learns to read exactly what he has written, not what he imagines to be there.

After he has read the work aloud, right through, he should have *heard* and *seen* some of his mistakes. Ask him to go back and correct them, with your help if necessary. Soon the corrections will become automatic, as he learns to stop the mistake.

When the child misses a mistake, pin-point it silently with your pencil. Ask him to read the word aloud *exactly* as he has written it; see if he can correct the spelling then.

Mistakes are often caused by lack of recall, due to the child's anxiety to get ideas and words down on paper as speedily as possible. Recall often comes when the piece is read *aloud*. See that the word is written down correctly and read aloud again, once the mistake has been 'spotted'.

The exercise 'spot the spelling mistake' is based on the all-purpose channels of *saying aloud*, and therefore also *hearing* and *seeing* the heard word in writing and so, hopefully, spotting the mistake. Then back through the channels of *seeing* the spelling mistake, *hearing* it correctly *aloud*, *writing* it correctly, *saying* it aloud again, and correspondingly *seeing* the correct image. Clear pronunciation of words aloud is an essential ingredient, followed by training the eye to really look, and the ear to give helpful clues; then the well organised brain stands a chance of recalling all the rules and regulations.

Example of ten single word spellings clearly dictated aloud to an intelligent 7 year old dyslexic boy. (Correct words have been added in small writing.) Note the difficulty with letter direction, discrimination between short vowels /a/ and /u/ and consonant blends. Also note the pen pressure and the /o/ starting at the bottom and looping round to the right, which will make cursive writing harder.

The Spelling Circle

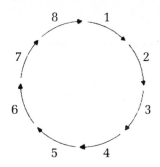

1 Clear pronunciation.

2 Word broken down into syllables.

3 Writing words down in syllables or parts.

4 Reading back aloud the written word.

5 Hearing and seeing the words.

6 Seeing omissions or mistakes.

7 Applying spelling rules.

8 Saying spellings out aloud.

READING EXERCISES

These exercises can be started once the child is reading a bit, that is to say, recognising letters strung together, but finding it hard to be fluent.

Sit together side by side. Choose a simple, clear print story book which you both enjoy. Practise each exercise for five minutes:

1 Quietly reading aloud *together*; you read steadily and smoothly, showing the place on the page with a marker. The child joins in as he can and gains the *feeling* of fluent reading. The flow of words off the printed page is something he needs to experience.

2 Quietly together, the child reads one word, you the next. This gives him a short rest after his word, but the fluency is continued by you. Mark the place on the page all the time.

3 Build up to reading aloud one sentence each. Swap over at each full stop. The child needs to rest his eyes, so he may look away but continue to listen. Keep the place clearly marked so that when he looks down he can immediately follow with his next sentence.

4 Gradually progress to one paragraph each, and later to a full page.

These reading exercises are designed to be carried out *aloud* to improve accuracy with fluency and to extend the experience of reading. Often this is all that is required to get a sticky reader running smoothly.

Reading with understanding is important, so ask the child to tell you *in his own words* what the story you have both been reading is all about, and to describe the meaning of some particular words to you. Reading with understanding may need lots of practice, but it can be both enjoyable and informative. Going back to repeat any of the procedures should be seen as necessary reinforcement, not as failure on the child's part or on yours.

Aim to practise building up the child's ability to tell a story in his own words once you have got the exercises under way. This link through from the spoken sentence to the written one, and the ability to read fluently comes about gradually, as the basic co-ordination, rhythm and timing patterns become established in the child's whole body movement.

EXERCISE SHEET 6 for POINTER 6.
Laterality.

You should know (from the tests in Pointer 6) which hand-eye-foot-side the child normally uses; or which needs strengthening to make it entirely dominant over the other. This dominant side can usually be judged according to which hand he writes with, but if in serious doubt, consult your doctor who will arrange for you and the child to see a neurologist, or paediatrician, who will test in depth.

EXERCISES TO STRENGTHEN 'ALL-ONE-SIDE'
LATERALITY

Eye and Hand

The child covers his non-dominant eye with his non-dominant hand (e.g. left hand over left eye, if the right hand and eye are to be encouraged to work strongly; *or* right hand over right eye, if the left hand and eye are to be strengthened).

The child extends his dominant arm straight in front of him. Place your outstretched index finger gently on the child's shoulder, and *slowly* travel down his arm to hand and fingertips. He watches this finger movement from start to finish.

Repeat once more.

Next day and every day for a few weeks, repeat the movement twice, always moving slowly and steadily down the child's arm.

Eye, Hand and Foot

Exercise 1 – Age Range: 6 Years Onwards.

On a big sheet of white card draw a large circle using a dustbin lid or similar shaped guide with a thick felt tip pen or crayon. Prop the card with the drawn circle upright against a chair or wall. The child, with shoes off, sits directly facing it and covers his non-dominant eye with his same-side hand. He puts his dominant hand comfortably over his same-side foot, and lifts his foot so that his toes touch the circle. Round and round *clockwise* he goes, his toes always touching the circle edge, hand in line with foot and the eye following around too. Slow, steady *accurate* movement is the aim. The child can stop when he has had enough of holding his foot off the ground.

Exercise 2 – Age Range: Specifically 6-11 Years.

Make a large drawing on light cardboard of the pattern (see below) with straight and curved lines, and place it upright on the floor against the wall. If the child is to remain left-handed then substitute 'left' for 'right' in the following sequence.

The child sits directly in front of the pattern with shoes off, and 'draws' it with:

- both feet held together.

- right foot only.

- right foot and right hand together.

- right foot and right eye consciously following the steady movements of the foot.

- right foot, hand and eye.

- both hands held together.

- right hand.

- right hand and right eye.

- right eye alone, looking along the pattern.

This exercise should be carried out two or three times weekly for as long as a year. More advanced exercises for children over the age of ten can be found in Audrey McAllen's book 'The Extra Lesson', and Exercises 1 and 2 given here are extracts from that book, with kind permission.

SIX SPECIFIC EXERCISES

Exercise 1 – Arm and Leg Movements with Jump.

This exercise stimulates co-ordination of upper and lower limbs and brings awareness of the possible diagonal positions of limbs on opposite sides of the body, as related to the child's symmetrical axis.

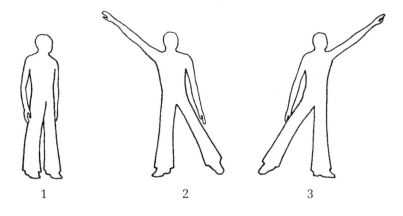

1   Starting position, feet together, arms at sides.

2   Stretch right arm diagonally up to right side, at same time stretch left leg diagonally out to left side.

3   Small jump to reverse position, now left arm stretched diagonally out to left side, right leg stretched diagonally out to right side.

4   5   6

4   *No* jump for return to starting position, left arm down, right leg back to centre.

5   Small jump, stretch both arms diagonally up at same time, feet apart, rest on toes.

6   *No* jump for return to starting position, both arms down, feet together (it does not matter which leg is moved to bring feet together, but one leg remains stationary).

Full Exercise: Repeat 1-6, eight times.

Exercise 2 – Crossways Walking.

This exercise forces the child to concentrate on his co-ordination, balance and especially foot movement. It should be done while looking firmly ahead (not at feet) as this encourages the child's proprioception (i.e. he has to know without looking what his feet are doing and where they are doing it).

On the floor draw a line at least 1 metre long or place a long ruler on the floor.

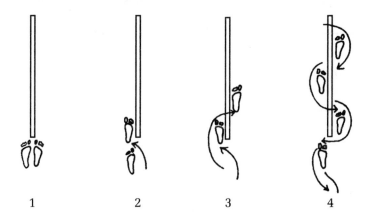

1   2   3   4

1 Stand at one end of line, feet together, arms resting at sides.

2 Step forward, right foot crossing over to left side of line.

3 Step forward, left foot crossing over to right side of line, in front of right foot. Continue to end of line.

4 Retrace steps moving backwards to starting point.

Exercise Progression

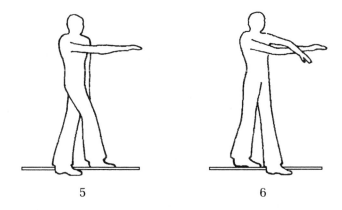

5   6

5 Stand as in 1, raise right arm to shoulder level, right arm and right foot cross over to left side.

6   Raise left arm, left arm and left foot cross over to right side, arms cross at shoulder level, left arm on top, elbows and wrists straight.

7   Continue to end of line then retrace steps back to starting point, feet and arms crossing under at each step, body upright.

Key Factor: Keep feet close to line without touching it, body upright.

Exercise 3 – Concentration Sequence.

This exercise consists of taking four even steps in a straight line in a large room, or, in a smaller room, to follow the curve of a large circle. The teacher counts: 1, 2, 3, 4. The child carries out a sequence of steps which involves stepping backward on one step of each group of 4. The step backwards changes position in each group of 4 of the sequence. This demands great concentration.

Diagram of Movement

~~1~~ 2   3   4

1   ~~2~~   3   4

1   2   ~~3~~   4

1   2   3   ~~4~~

~~1~~   2   3   4

(The crossed out numbers denotes the backward step & clap.)

Starting position. The step backwards is a token step, i.e. rock on back step, always lead forward with the other foot.

a) One step back on count 1, three steps forward on count 2, 3, 4 (i.e. *back* 2, 3, 4).

b) One step forward on count 1, one step back on count 2, two steps forward on count 3, 4 (i.e. 1, *back*, 3, 4).

c) Two steps forward on count 1, 2, one step back on count 3, one step forward on 4 (i.e. 1, 2, *back*, 4).

d) Three steps forward on count 1, 2, 3, one step back on count 4 (i.e. 1, 2, 3, *back*).

The sequence is now completed. Restart from a): *back* 2, 3, 4, and so on.

Note, at this point *only*, two steps back are taken.

Exercise Progression

a) When the stepping has been mastered the child may clap once on the backward step, and the teacher count "Clap, 2, 3, 4".

b) Next the teacher can say "1, 2, 3, 4" and emphasise the number on which the clap and backward step are taken.

c) Finally the exercise can be done silently.

Key Factor: Start with feet together. The feet *never* come together again in this exercise.

Exercise 4 – Expand and Contract.

The important feature of this exercise is the repeated movement of expansion and contraction. This must not be abrupt and pointed but a gradual oscillation between centre and periphery, with distance first increasing and then decreasing. The teacher could usefully suggest to the child the image of the tide filling a cave, with water entering more and more deeply in a succession of waves.

When the exercise is first introduced the teacher should count out loud to maintain the rhythm; she should, however, aim at eventually doing the exercise silently since the stepping involved in the combined foot and upper body movements contains the rhythm.

When the actual movements have been mastered individually, the teacher can introduce, in a classroom situation, the element of group expansion and contraction with teacher and children standing together in a circle. Alternatively, the teacher or a child can be the still focal point at the centre of the circle, the others moving rhythmically inwards and outwards.

1

1   Starting position. Feet together, arms loosely at sides.

2   Leading with the right foot, take:
   • 1 step forward.
   • 2 steps backward.
   • 3 steps forward.
   • 4 steps backward.
   • 5 steps forward.
   • 6 steps backward.

3   Then take:
   • 5 steps forward.
   • 4 steps backward.
   • 3 steps forward.
   • 2 steps backward.
   • 1 step forward, with feet together as in starting position.

Key Factor: The right foot leads whenever there is a change of direction, rocking on the left. When there is a change of direction, count 1 on the right foot.

1   2   3

Exercise Progression

1   Starting position for movements of upper part of body.

2   Counting 1. Hands to chest, fingers curled, knuckles on chest, head and back slightly bowed.

3   Counting 1, 2. Upper arms remain close to body, forearms and hands slightly open out, fingers half uncurl, palms face each other, head up, back straight.

4   5   6   7

4   Counting 1, 2, 3. Hands to chest, fingers curled, knuckles on chest, head and back curled up as in 1, but more so.

5   Counting 1, 2, 3, 4. Upper arms move away from body, elbows flexed, forearms and hands open out, palms upward, fingers uncurl, head and back lean slightly backwards.

6 Counting 1, 2, 3, 4, 5. Hands to chest as in 1 and 3, head well down, back well rounded, knees slightly flexed.

7 Counting 1, 2, 3, 4, 5, 6. Arms raised up and out from shoulders, palms face upwards, fingers uncurl, head and back lean well backwards.

8 Reverse order of exercise. Repeat 5, then 4, 3, 2 and 1, and back to starting position.

Further Exercise Progression

1   2   3

Starting position for combined movements of whole body.

1 Starting position.

2 Counting 1. Take one step forward, hands to chest, fingers curled, knuckles on chest, head and back slightly bowed.

3 Counting 1, 2. Take 2 steps backward, repeat 2 above.

4 Continue the exercise, joining foot to upper body movements through 3, 4, 5 and 6. Then reverse order, do 5, 4, 3, 2, 1 back to starting position.

Exercise 5 – Spiral in Space.

In this exercise the teacher could usefully suggest to the child the image of a snail curling up inside the shell, or climbing up a spiral staircase to the top of a tower. By following imaginatively and physically the spiral form, the child experiences one complete continuous movement, rather than related fragments. For a child who has difficulty in completing a story, sentence or train of thought this exercise may initially be difficult. When mastery of the exercise has resulted in a relaxed flow of movement, the movement can be speeded up to a run.

Before starting the exercise, the teacher must say:

"Do you know what a spiral is?" (If the child does not know then the teacher must explain).

Pretend there is a spiral on the floor in front of you. You will follow the line of the spiral clockwise to the centre then reverse out of the spiral, walking backwards anti-clockwise. (If the child does not know the meaning of 'clockwise', the teacher will again have to explain.)

1   2

1 Stand feet together, arms open in wide V above head, palms facing inwards, head and body leaning slightly backwards.

2 Walk clockwise into centre of spiral, gradually drawing downwards and inwards.

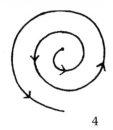

3

4

3   At centre, crouched and tucked position, head bowed, fingers curled close to chest.

4   Walk backwards anti-clockwise out of spiral, gradually expanding, straightening out arms stretching upwards, back to position 1.

Full Exercise: Repeat 1-4, three times.

Exercise 6 – Moving in a Figure of '8' (Eight).

This exercise involves moving without pause from one position to the next, maintaining a smooth continuous rhythm and a *forward facing position, with the whole body facing point X throughout.*

The length of the straight line should fit the available space. Draw it, label it ABC, emphasise B, which is the crossing point. Mark X on the wall, or a piece of furniture. The exercise can be done to music or a rhyme, for example, 'I had a little nut tree', which the child must say aloud.

Straight lines

I had a little nut tree	walk forward A to C
Nothing would it bear	walk backward C to A
But a silver nutmeg	walk forward A to C
And a golden pear.	walk backward C to A

Curved lines

The King of Spain's daughter	walk A to B (curved right line to centre)
Came to visit me,	walk B to C (curved line to left)
And all for the sake	walk C to B (curve right)
Of my little nut tree.	walk B to A (curve left, back to beginning)

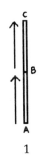
1

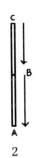
2

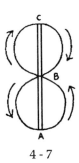
4 - 7

1   Walk forward along straight line, A to C.

2   Using same number of steps, walk backwards along straight line C to A.

3   Repeat 1 and 2 once.

4   Now back at A, *still facing X*, walk round forwards along first curve to the right.

5   Now at B, *still facing X*, walk round forwards along second curve to the left.

6   Now at C, *still facing X*, walk round backwards along third curve to the right.

7   Now back at B, *still facing X*, walk round backwards along fourth curve to the left.

Full Exercise: Repeat 1-7, three times.

Key Factor: Face point X throughout.

SECTION E

Useful Contacts and Further Reading

MAINLY FOR PARENTS
Organisations Providing Information, Support or Training.

ATTENTION DEFICIT DISORDER INFORMATION
AND SUPPORT SERVICE (ADDISS)
10 Station Road, Mill Hill, London NW7 2JU.
Helpline: 020 8906 9068
E-mail: info@addiss.co.uk
www.addiss.co.uk

*Information and support on
Attention Deficit Hyperactivity Disorder.*

ADVISORY CENTRE FOR EDUCATION ('ACE') LTD
1c Aberdeen Studios, 22 Highbury Grove, London N5 2DQ.
Helpline: 0808 800 5793
E-mail: ace-ed@easynet.org.uk
www.ace-ed.org.uk

*Provides information on all aspects of education for parents
and teachers through their magazine, 'Where'. ACE can also
answer individual questions on education.*

ASSOCIATION FOR ALL SPEECH IMPAIRED CHILDREN
('AFASIC')
2nd Floor, 50-52 Great Sutton Street, London EC1V 0DJ.
Helpline: 0845 355 5577
E-mail: info@afasic.org.uk
www.afasic.org.uk

*Representing children and young people with speech and
language difficulties. Support, information and local groups.*

ASSOCIATION OF EURYTHMY THERAPISTS
Rudolf Steiner House, 35 Park Road, London NW1 6XT.
Helpline: 0207 723 4400
E-mail: rsh@cix.compulink.co.uk

Courses, contacts, information.

ASSOCIATION OF SPEECH AND LANGUAGE THERAPISTS
IN INDEPENDENT PRACTICE ('ASLTIP')
WSS, Coleheath Bottom, Speen, Princes Risborough,
Buckinghamshire HP27 0SZ.
Helpline: 0870 241 3357
Medico-Legal Helpline: 0870 241 2068
E-mail: asltip@awdry.demon.co.uk
www.helpwithtalking.com

BRAIN GYM INTERNATIONAL
E-mail: info@braingym.org.uk
www.braingym.org.uk

BRITISH ASSOCIATION OF BEHAVIOURAL
OPTOMETRISTS ('BABO')
72 High Street, Billericay, Essex CM12 9BS.
Helpline: 01277 624916
E-mail: aquilla72@aol.com
www.assoc-optometrists.org
Register of accredited optometrists throughout the UK.

BRITISH DYSLEXIA ASSOCIATION ('BDA')
98 London Road, Reading, Berkshire RG1 5AU.
Helpline: 0118 966 8271
E-mail: info@dyslexia-bda.demon.co.uk
www.bda-dyslexia.org.uk
*Leaflets available, plus contact address of your nearest local
Dyslexia Association affiliated to the BDA; courses for teachers
and therapists; lectures list; counselling and advisory service.*

CONTACT A FAMILY
209-211 City Road, London EC1V 1JN.
Helpline: 0808 808 3555
E-mail: info@cafamily.org.uk
www.cafamily.org.uk

DYSLEXIA INSTITUTE
Park House, Wick Road, Egham, Surrey TW20 0HH.
Helpline: 01784 222300
E-mail: info@dyslexia-inst.org.uk
www.dyslexia-inst.org.uk
*Assessment and tuition for children with specific learning
difficulties in nearly 50 teaching 'outposts' throughout the
country. Annual edition of 'Parents Handbook'. Courses for
teachers at diploma and MA level.*

DYSPRAXIA FOUNDATION
8 West Alley, Hitchin, Hertfordshire SG5 1EG.
Helpline: 01462 454 986
E-mail: admin@dyspraxiafoundation.org.uk
www.dyspraxiafoundation.org.uk
*To promote diagnosis, treatment, understanding and
recognition of dyspraxia and its implications.*

EDUCATION OTHERWISE
PO Box 7420, London N9 9SG.
Helpline: 0870 730 0074
E-mail: enquiries@education-otherwise.org
www.education-otherwise.org
Information about home-based education.

HELEN ARKELL DYSLEXIA CENTRE
Mill Bridge, Frensham, Farnham, Surrey GU10 3BW.
Helpline: 01252 792400
E-mail: enquiries@arkellcentre.org.uk
www.arkellcentre.org.uk
Teacher training, courses, assessment and advice on dyslexia.

HORNSBY INTERNATIONAL DYSLEXIA CENTRE
Wye Street, London SW11 2HB.
Helpline: 0207 223 1144
E-mail: dyslexia@hornsby.co.uk
www.hornsby.co.uk
Accredited training courses in teaching dyslexia for qualified teachers and others. Short, update and distance learning courses. Information, books and software.

HYPERACTIVE CHILDREN'S SUPPORT GROUP
71 Whyke Lane, Chichester, West Sussex PO19 7PD.
Helpline: 01243 551313
E-mail: contact@hacsg.org.uk
www.hacsg.org.uk
Information for parents and professional resource pack.

I CAN
4 Dyer's Buildings, Holborn, London EC1N 2QP.
Helpline: 0870 010 4066/0845 225 4071
E-mail: ican@ican.org.uk
www.ican.org.uk
Help and advice for families of children with speech, language and communication difficulties; links to specialist support bodies.

INTERNATIONAL STRESS MANAGEMENT
ASSOCIATION ('ISMA')
PO Box 348, Waltham Cross, Hertfordshire EN8 8ZL.
Helpline: 07000 780 430
E-mail: stress@isma.org.uk
www.isma.org.uk
Advice on where to seek help locally.

'IPSEA' (Independent Panel for Special Education Advice)
6 Carlow Mews, Woodbridge, Suffolk IP12 1EA.
Helpline England and Wales: 0800 018 4016
Scotland: 0131 454 0082
N. Ireland: 01232 705654
www.ipsea.org.uk

Guides parents through the assessment (statementing) and tribunal procedures.

NATIONAL AUTISTIC SOCIETY ('NAS')
393 City Road, London EC1V 1NG.
Helpline: 0870 6008585
E-mail: autismhelpline@nas.org.uk
www.autism.co.uk

Specialist schools, diagnosis, assessment, service, information, courses and conferences.

PATOSS – PROFESSIONAL ASSOCIATION OF TEACHERS
OF STUDENTS WITH SPECIFIC LEARNING DIFFICULTIES
PO Box 10, Evesham, Worcestershire WR11 1ZW.
Helpline: 01386 712650
E-mail: patoss@evesham.ac.uk
www.patoss-dyslexia.org

Newsletter, local contact.

ROYAL COLLEGE OF SPEECH AND LANGUAGE
THERAPISTS
2 White Hart Yard, London SE1 1NX.
Helpline: 0207 378 1200
E-mail: postmaster@rcslt.org
www.rcslt.org

Information, leaflets, contacts, courses and overseas listings about speech, language and voice disorders in all ages.

TRAINING FOR CURATIVE EURYTHMY
Peredur Centre for Arts, Dunnings Road, East Grinstead,
West Sussex RH19 4NF.
Helpline: 01342 312527

MAINLY FOR TEACHERS AND THERAPISTS

Suppliers of Teaching Resources and Publications – On-line and Catalogue Service.

BETTER BOOKS
3 Paganel Drive, Dudley, West Midlands DY1 4AZ.
Helpline: 01384 253276
E-mail: enquiries@betterbooks.com
www.betterbooks.com

BRAINWORKS
Helpline: 08705 143053
www.brainworks.co.uk
Wide range of learning resources on-line.

LEARNING DEVELOPMENT AIDS (LDA)
Duke Street, Wisbech, Cambridgeshire PE13 2AE.
Helpline: 01945 463441
www.ldalearning.com
Catalogues of educational material and games.

NFER-NELSON
Unit 28, Bramble Road, Techno Trading Estate, Swindon, Wiltshire SN2 8EZ.
Helpline: 0208 996 8445
Customer service: 0845 602 1937
E-mail: information@nfer-nelson.co.uk
www.nfer-nelson.co.uk

PLAYRING LTD
53 Westbere Road, West Hampstead, London NW2 3SP.
Helpline: 0207 794 9497
Award winning activity/play toys and materials.

ROMPA
Goyt Side Road, Chesterfield, Derbyshire S40 2PH.
Helpline: 0800 056 2323
E-mail: sales@rompa.com
www.rompa.com
A wide range of resources for special needs, mainstream education and therapy work.

SPECIAL EDUCATIONAL NEEDS MARKETING
618 Leeds Road, Outwood, Wakefield WF1 2LT.
Helpline: 01924 871697
E-mail: sen.marketing@ukonline.co.uk
www.sen.uk.com

Books and other resources for special needs, especially dyslexia.

SPEECHMARK PUBLISHING LTD
Telford Road, Bicester, Oxfordshire OX26 4LQ.
Helpline: 01869 244644 / 244733
E-mail: janj@speechamrk.net
www.speechmark.net

Specialist resource material, 'ColorCards', early skills, augmentative communication.

STASS PUBLICATIONS
44 North Road, Ponteland, Northumberland NE20 9UR.
Helpline: 01661 822 316
E-mail: susan@stass.demon.co.uk
www.stasspublications.co.uk

All materials are designed, written and produced by speech and language therapists.

TASKMASTER LTD
Morris Road, Leicester LE2 6BR.
Helpline: 0116 270 4286
E-mail: info@taskmasteronline.co.uk
www.taskmasteronline.co.uk

Materials for speech, language, hearing, special needs, mathematics.

THE PSYCHOLOGICAL CORPORATION
32 Jamestown Road, London NW1 7BY.
Helpline: 01865 888 188
E-mail: tpc@harcourt.com
www.tpc-international.com

SUGGESTED FURTHER READING

Most organisations listed provide information through leaflets and other publications, and on-line – go to their websites for details. A wide range of titles is available from specialist distributors – such as Better Books and Special Educational Needs Marketing.

ALPHA TO OMEGA
B. Hornsby, F. Shear and J. Pool
Heinemann Educational Books   ISBN 0-435104-233

A-Z of teaching, reading, writing and spelling.

DAY-TO-DAY DYSLEXIA IN THE CLASSROOM
J. Pollock and E. Walker
Routledge   ISBN 0-415111-323

Offers advice to teachers on how they can recognise SpLD and gives practical help to children in the class.

DYSLEXIA AND MATHEMATICS
edited by T. R. and E. Miles
Routledge   ISBN 0-415049-873

A collection of contributions from six practitioners in the field of teaching dyslexic children of all ages.

HEAR IT, SEE IT, SAY IT, DO IT – Books 1, 2, 3 & 4
Mary Atkinson
Cheerful Publications   ISBN 1-872432-018

A structural aid to teaching, reading, writing and spelling for parents and teachers (including instructions, worksheets and games to cut out – in four different books – photocopiable).

HOW TO IDENTIFY AND SUPPORT CHILDREN WITH
SPEECH AND LANGUAGE DIFFICULTIES
Jane Speake
LDA   ISBN 1-85503-361-5

Help for teachers in the classroom.

KEEPING A HEAD IN SCHOOL
Dr. M. D. Levine (USA)
Educators Publishing Service   ISBN 0-838820-697

A student's book about learning abilities and learning disorders.

LEFT-HANDER'S HANDBOOK, THE
Diane G Paul
The Robinswood Press   ISBN 1-869981-596

The guide for parents and teachers to help left-handed children in a right-handed world.

OVERCOMING DYSLEXIA
B. Hornsby
Vermilion – Prospect House   ISBN 0-091813-204

A straightforward guide for families and teachers.

TITLES FROM THE ROBINSWOOD PRESS

*SPOTLIGHT ON WORDS Books One and Two

Phonic wordsearch puzzles and activities.

Gillian Aitken

Wordsearch puzzles and fill-in-the-blank activities to help in the development of spelling skills. Each puzzle is based on a specific vowel or sound combination. So these books can be used by teachers as part of a structured approach to spelling and to concentrate learning activity where it is needed most. For pupils, the puzzles provide both enjoyment and a challenge, a thoroughly satisfying way to learn.

The puzzles are appropriate for ages 9 to 12 years and beyond. Clear design guides the reader's eye and the hidden words only run across or down making both *Spotlight on Words* books an excellent resource for dyslexic pupils.

ISBN: 1-869981-510 (Book 1)
ISBN: 1-869981-731 (Book 2)   £16.95 each

*SPOTLIGHT ON BLENDS Books One and Two

Phonic activities on initial (Book One) and end (Book Two) consonant blends to improve spelling skills, reading accuracy and phonological awareness.

Gillian Aitken

The worksheets in these titles give systematic practice of consonant blends. The main emphasis is on developing phonological awareness by means of sound blending, rhyming and careful contrasting of blends which are similar in sound. Research shows that training in such skills leads to improved reading accuracy and spelling.

The worksheets have a clear, uncluttered visual layout which will enable many pupils to work independently. However, detailed teaching notes and guidelines accompany the worksheets.

ISBN: 1-869981-553 (Book 1)
ISBN: 1-869981-531 (Book 2)   £16.95 each

---

*SPOTLIGHT ON SUFFIXES Books One and Two

Common Suffixes and Suffixing Rules. Years 1 to 5 (Book One).

Suffix Recognition and Use, Spelling Rules, Grammar and Vocabulary. Years 4 to 8 (Book Two – Key Stage 3).

Gillian Aitken

The worksheets are a useful complement to any structured literacy programme, improving spelling skills as well as raising language awareness in general, particularly in the area of grammar and word meanings.

ISBN: 1-869981-60X (Book 1)
ISBN: 1-869981-618 (Book 2)   £16.95 each

*PHONIC RHYME TIME

A unique collection of phonic rhymes for precise practice in speaking and reading.

Mary Nash-Wortham

Phonic Rhyme Time solves the problem of finding memorable rhymes which concentrate solely on one specific sound. Many traditional rhymes contain similar sounds that are in reality significantly different, leading to considerable confusion. In contrast, every rhyme and verse in *Phonic Rhyme Time* has been selected or created because it is dedicated to just one precise sound. The wide range of rhymes means it is suitable for both children and adults. The clear presentation enables easy selection and varied use of the rhymes.

ISBN: 1-869981-472   £16.95

LEFT-HANDER'S HANDBOOK

Diane G. Paul

An essential guide for teachers, teachers' trainers and parents of left-handed children. Highly commended Runner-up in 1999 BMA Medical Book Competition.

ISBN: 1-869981-596   £11.95

*THE LIFEBOAT SCHEME

Sula Ellis, Tony Ellis, Jackie Davison, Mick Davison

Launch the Lifeboat to Read and Spell is a self-contained, highly-structured literacy scheme, suitable for all students, particularly those with specific learning difficulties. Each of ten books contains ten lessons and each lesson is made up of eight photocopiable worksheets. The worksheets are consistent throughout and provide exercises whose main features are:

- reading for meaning; visual perceptive skills; hand-eye co-ordination.

- visual recognition.

- phonological awareness; visual and auditory skills; writing.

- reading and comprehension.

- dictation; cursive handwriting; memory training; proof-reading; kinaesthetic memory.

- listening skills.

- comprehension and writing; cloze procedure.

- visual screening.

"It gives me great pleasure to commend this Resource Pack. I know it to be based on the authors' many years' experience in the teaching of dyslexic children and on their knowledge of what these children are likely to find difficult. Moreover, this pack so obviously represents good practice that one can recommend it as being suitable for teaching reading and spelling to all children, whether dyslexic or not".

From the Foreword by Professor T. R. Miles.

ISBN: 1-869981-723   10-Book Set £164.50 (£16.95 per Book).

---

*These books are spiral bound. The publisher permits copying for use within one establishment.

Books from The Robinswood Press are available through book stockists, educational distributors, and direct via the website below or by using the photocopiable order form.

www.robinswoodpress.com

PHOTOCOPIABLE ORDER FORM

For direct purchase send to address below.
Please allow 28 days for delivery.

Title and ISBN 1-869981-		No. of copies	Price per Book	Total
Eurythmy	480		£2.95	
Lifeboat Book 1	626		£16.95	
Lifeboat Book 2	634		£16.95	
Lifeboat Book 3	642		£16.95	
Lifeboat Book 4	650		£16.95	
Lifeboat Book 5	669		£16.95	
Lifeboat Book 6	677		£16.95	
Lifeboat Book 7	685		£16.95	
Lifeboat Book 8	693		£16.95	
Lifeboat Book 9	707		£16.95	
Lifeboat Book 10	715		£16.95	
Lifeboat 10-Book Set	723		£164.50	
Phonic Rhyme Time	472		£16.95	
Spotlight on Blends Book 1	553		£16.95	
Spotlight on Blends Book 2	561		£16.95	
Spotlight on Suffixes Book 1	60X		£16.95	
Spotlight on Suffixes Book 2	618		£16.95	
Spotlight on Words Book 1	510		£16.95	
Spotlight on Words Book 2	731		£16.95	
Take Time	588		£11.95	
The Left-hander's Handbook	596		£11.95	

UK Postage & Packing   1 book £1.95. 2 books £4.30.
3+ books £6.95. Orders over £175.00 post free.

I enclose a cheque made payable to
The Robinswood Press,

TOTAL £ [   ]

or: charge my VISA or MasterCard, number [   ]

Name on card [   ]   Expiry Date [   ]

Name [   ]   Date [   ]

Address [   ]

[   ]   Postcode [   ]

Phone [   ]   Signature [   ]

The Robinswood Press South Avenue Stourbridge West Midlands DY8 3XY
Telephone: 01384 397475   Fax: 01384 440443
E-mail: info@robinswoodpress.com   Web site: www.robinswoodpress.com